Foragers:
A Dangerous Pastime

Jayke Luland

First published by Busybird Publishing 2025

ISBN: Print: 978-1-923216-75-4
          Ebook: 978-1-923216-76-1

This is a work of fiction. Any similarities between places and characters are a coincidence.

Cover image: Danielle Evercroft

Cover design: Busybird Publishing

Layout and typesetting: Busybird Publishing

Busybird Publishing
2/118 Para Road
Montmorency, Victoria
Australia 3094
www.busybird.com.au

Contents

Weed in the Grass

'I don't like her,' said the man in the Amadou hat, perched inside a children's playground at a small Tumut park.

'Me neither,' said an unkempt woman as she slid down a slide and scurried behind the barricade where this man was nestled. Her cobweb-covered binoculars jangled from her neck, spiders flying everywhere. 'She exudes malevolence.'

Jim peered into his periscope with a degree of trepidation. 'A penchant for violence.'

'Evil incarnate.'

It was a late afternoon, and the cicadas were chirping as the light of the bright May day was fading. As the night began to open its eyes, these intrepid travellers anticipated a different type of forthcoming darkness.

The man – twirling the end of his moustache – turned to the woman with a frown. He pondered for a moment, moving his hand down to his soul patch, caressing it like he was caring for a dying house plant. His soft caress, despite the toxicity of the tree sap on his hand, sprung his stubbly facial hair to life, which couldn't be said when he would touch and sing to his succulents.

'She's up to something nefarious.' The man peered through the barrel of his periscope, casting his steely disdain upon this no-goodnik. With spades in their pockets and infringement notices ready, they were ready to shirtfront this lady without mercy.

'Good lord, she's unbelievable!' said the woman, face contorted. 'Mixing mustard greens and eucalyptus leaves? She must be some sort of animal!'

'Her and her ill-gotten gains,' the man replied, chewing on a dirty old mushroom, speckles of dirt still lingering in his dry mouth like the grounds of a bitter Turkish Coffee.

'She's nestling her burdock root into the same bag as her nettle, that's a disaster waiting to happen!'

'What sort of amateur-hour hoodlums are we letting into this area?'

'The scrounge of society, that's who.'

'Ne'er do wells.'

'Belligerent ballyhoos.' The two pulled themselves away from their scopes. They jotted down several notes and observations in a small flower-shaped children's booklet with cuddly tigers on the front. In the eyes of the law they adhere to, their case was made.

This was Jimothy and Shelly; lovers and co-presidents of *Urban Foragers Tumut*. They were charged with maintaining the stringent codes and ethics surrounding the antediluvian practice of Urban Foraging. With the dangers of their semi-profession often weighing on the minds of its members, Jim and Shelly ensured the broader community was kept safe from the derelicts that scavenged these parts for a bit of booty. Marauders, miscreants and madlads often roamed the outskirts, looking for a way into this quaint community. To the unlearned and unkempt, Jimothy and Shelly were the iron wall of courage foragers needed to survive in this increasingly brutal society.

This was why 21-year-old Faye Friendly posed such a threat. An upstanding community member by day, she had the gumption to enter this community without permission from the powers that be. She had been looking for fresh local produce to acquire in a community-driven initiative she'd been involved in. A bubbly, whimsical figure within Tumut, many saw her as a lovely young girl who wanted to give back to her community. An effervescent lass who'd help an old woman cross the street or a close friend move, Faye was a model citizen that many of her peers aspired to be.

Jim and Shelly saw evil in her eyes, however. A woman who so recklessly foraged these forests was not to be trusted. Her various infractions caused great distress within this tight-knitted community; Jim and Shelly heard many complaints from foragers ranging in scale from ridiculously petty to slightly inconveniencing.

For instance, she'd been sighted on several occasions not using the proper South Peruvian twisting technique to harvest her greens. Another gripe made by one anonymous source alleged that Faye had left food crumbs on the ground, an infringement that'd seen people hanged in a more barbaric time. She'd even gone as far as over-harvesting her nettles, which was a needle in the eye of anyone with a bit of approbation. While most would see this as an innocent mistake from a fly-by-day delinquent, Jim and Shelly saw this as a declaration of war.

Much in the same way that local dog walker Blake saw this as a bit odd. Noticing these oddly dressed characters gawking over the blithesome young lass, he politely inquired.

'Oi, what's going on gang?' His pit bull sniffed at the feet of these two wayward wayfarers. The spritely mutt lit up as she stood at attention, something fishy was in the air, and it wasn't just the half-eaten fish and chips strewn over a nearby park bench.

This concern was certainly not walleyed by the response.

'Exercising jurisprudence over the scum of society, my friend,' Jim replied, 'the scum of society.' Looking longingly out into the distance as if he'd said something remotely profound, Jim chuckled to himself. A man with great pride in what he did, he considered himself as a noble figure who'd obtained great influence in society. His jurisprudence over the ecosystem was the only thing keeping the climate crisis at bay, as he so often claimed. Needless to say, a man patrolling the forest of Tumut could not alone stop the existential threat of climate change.

Blake looked Jim up and down, his eyes investigating Jim's cavernous wrinkles like a crime scene. 'Right …' he said with a snicker, 'looks to me like you're havin' a perv on Faye there, champion.'

Jim went red in the face, clammy in the hands and stammered for a response to these most inflammatory accusations. The beads of sweat on his face felt like concrete, enveloped by the weight of it all. He was known to be a little self-conscious about how he was perceived by the greater public. He wanted to be a respected figure within Tumut, not a freak show that people avoided. These types of interactions didn't help his case.

'Uh, buh, buh, duh … how dare you.' Jim's voice was raised, his rather harsh inflections typical of a man caught in a trap. 'You licentious lurch, how dare you make such sensationalist insinuations!'

By this point, Jim's overly large schnoz was firmly implanted in the face of the dog walker; a threatening sight if he weren't dressed in suspenders, a white button down and an Amadou hat. With Jim rubbing his forefinger along the cold metal of the high-grade peashooter in his back pocket, a brouhaha was brewing.

'If I were you, I'd get back.' Shelly opened her fanny-pack, ready to release her self-defensive nettle net designed to sting your socks off. A small deployable bag filled with nettles was a common weapon in the arsenal of your typical Urban Forager, often deployed to ward off suspicious swindlers or devious dacoits. For many, the content inside Shelly's fanny often stuck with them for the long run, causing various health problems along the way.

'Layabout,' Jim snarled, earthy, worm-laced spit spraying into the face of this humble dog walker. The smallest bit of blood was emitted in his spit, which would've caused concern if he wasn't so focused on warding off this suspicious stroll-along. His wild plant-based diet was something that could lead to serious issues vis-à-vis liver disease and cancer. However, certain predispositions about western medicine caused him to avoid the doctor like the plague; ironic when you consider his brushes with various contagions.

'Jeez, steady on champion,' Blake replied, backing up despite the muffled growl of his pit bull. Blake was focused on grabbing his pizza and settling in for a night of video games. A stoush with these two was not on the agenda.

Realising that this whole incident may have come across as a bit tense, Jimothy stood down and offered a truce. Reaching into his tote bag, he fumbled around for a brief second – pricking himself on a couple of indiscernible thorns – before pulling out a whole bunch of yellow-capped mushrooms.

In times of distress, a handful of mushrooms could soothe quite a number of tricky situations. A basketful of yellow caps was infamously given as a peace offering by Dictator Callum the Tsar from Zanzibar to quell rising tensions with Saint Helena President Rodri Boris. Peace had been achieved for several minutes before Rodri began spewing up a vile viscus, dying only minutes later. Needless to say, peacetime was over, and the great Zanzibar-Saint Helena War of 2004 waged on.

Blake took the mushrooms and Jim apologised. 'I'm sorry, the task of policing illegal foraging is a tough business, son. I offer these mushies as a token of truce, a sign of my sorrow. They go great in Ratatouille, my intrepid young fellow!'

'Grate them and slice them,' Shelly added.

'Dice them and splice them,' Jim said.

Diplomacy wasn't always possible in Tumut, so this was a nice change of pace from the decades-long power struggles the town was known for. The concept of a mayor going missing or foragers waging war wasn't foreign to Tumut, but Blake had seemingly avoided such trivialities.

'Righto, cheers gang.' Blake nestled the mushrooms into his right pocket. 'Steady on fellas, aye?' The man slowly backed away, giving a gentle tug on Pablo's collar before heading onto pastures new, hopefully far away from these oddsters. Having dealt with one threat in a swift fashion, the two were now ready to teach young Faye a lesson in proper foraging practices. As Faye hummed a melodic tune to herself, a war was slowly rising out of the trenches like the sun on a crisp Autumn morning in 1915.

Wayward Travellers

Returning from the forest with a basket full of goodies, Faye arrived at the local farmer's market. Having picked a whole bundle of flowers, she'd organised them by colour and bunched them into bouquets. Selling each bouquet for $5 a pop, all profits from these flowers were intended to go towards the local charity *BagABetterLife*, a not-for-profit focused on delivering school bags for underprivileged kids in the Snowy Valleys.

It was an hour into this event and her self-sourced flowers were a hit. She'd sold 19 bouquets to a few loving couples. With love in the air and a sparkle in the eyes of Tumutians everywhere, Faye's flowers were a welcome presence that added a pop of colour to the dreary old hall.

Often regarded as the Paris of Regional New South Wales, Tumut was a place where Cupid's arrow pierced the murky depths of even the most cast-iron heart. The beau ideals of the Snowy's were considered the perfect partners for any members of the lonely-hearts club. True crime aficionados often kept a close eye on the town, eager for a jilted lovers' revenge story to arise. Alas, they would be waiting a while, as the Snowy's were too beautiful a place for murderers to congregate. They often chose a more decadent and depraved town, with less colour and more gentrification such as Wagga Wagga.

As she wove a chaplet, she noticed an odd-looking couple watching her from the entrance of the hall. They were old, weary types dressed rather strangely. They were trying to look inconspicuous, but their fleeting glances caught the curious eye of young Faye. What were these strangers doing here? What did they want?

This also caught the eye of local shoe smith Fannie de Hamza. The 70-year-old woman was a little bit senile and constantly paranoid; she regularly accused her customers of trying to ignite a Marxist revolution against her famed *Clog Your Heart* store on Wynyard Street. Her fear of the workers of the world uniting caused an unfortunately high turnover rate within her store. The suspicious glare of these two wayward wayfarers caused her paranoia to heighten, and in her elevated state of distress, she decided to share these concerns with Faye.

'Addison, I have a bad feeling about those no goodniks.' Unfortunately, Fannie was in such a state of mental decline that she'd often struggle to remember the names of many Tumutians. Faye was no exception.

'Yeah, they keep looking over at us,' Faye remarked, sitting a little bit more upright in her chair, then shuffled. Despite their best efforts to blend into the scenery, these two were a bit too obvious. If they were private investigators, the case would be lost and they'd be on the street singing suey for a sandwich. Their private eyes were a bit too public.

'I'm telling you Addy, the Marxists are here and they're trying to take my kicks.'

Faye decided not to correct Fannie, feeling she'd be a bit uptight to get hung up on a misremembered name. She was also weary of getting in the trenches on political matters. Fannie was a prominent voice within the local Submergist Movement lobbying to submerge Tumut and create an underwater kingdom called Tapat. She would wax lyrical for hours on end about the Marxist plot to dismantle *Clog Your Heart* and make the good people on Tumut live in the piercing agony of land-faring life. As a relatively apolitical young woman,

Faye wisely decided not to wade through such choppy waters, for the sake of both her sanity and diplomatic stability within Tumut.

At that moment, the two wayward wayfarers made a most fatal mistake: direct eye contact. Their sunken, weathered eyes locked steady with the effervescent green goggles of young Faye. It was quite the awkward moment, both parties wanting to look away, but also wanting to suss the other out. Those five seconds seemed like five days; five days that felt like five years.

Feeling accosted from a distance, the two wayward wayfarers quickly scurried out of the hall, bumping into an older man and knocking him flat on his arse. The whole situation was a strange one. What did these folks want? Were they nervous old creeps wanting to have a dalliance? It was a fleeting, yet uneasy encounter.

Faye looked out into the distance for a brief second, before getting a grip of herself and focusing on the bouquet. Unfortunately, while distracted, some fleet-fingered felon had nicked a stray Dandelion that'd been resting on her desk. Before she could properly react, she'd seen her culprit trapped under an irate Fannie de Hamza.

'Damn you, you landfarin' ass!' Despite her age, Fannie had managed to apprehend an Irish traveller, the most constant source of thievery and malfeasance.

The traveller had scraggly hair, missing teeth, and a 'KEEP TUMUT AFLOAT' shirt on. In a town low on crime but high on morale, criminals seldom roamed the streets of Tumut. Nor did they make such a bold political statement.

'I was just looking for a wee flower for me lassie,' said the Irish traveller, struggling for breath as Fannie's rear end rested on his sternum. The presence of Irish travellers in Tumut often took the air out of any room they happened to be in. In a way, this was welcome revenge for the effect they'd had on many of the town's most cherished events.

With the man subdued and a zip tie quickly placed around his ankles, Fannie turned to Faye. She had a look of concern for the traveller, emblematic of her affection for all of God's creatures. Even for those wishing to relieve her of her goods, she'd still give them the shirt off her back to make them feel a bit better. It made for a nice little Depop hustle for one lady that Faye had donated clothes to: raking in several hundred dollars from her hand-me-downs.

'Wanna take this prick to the cops, Addie?' Fannie asked, her forearm resting on the back of the Irish traveller's neck, threatening to cut off circulation.

'Nah, just let him go. He won't try that twice.' With a huge sigh, Fannie stood up and let the traveller go on his merry way. Faye didn't want trouble. No matter what happened, she just wanted to keep the peace, not a piece in her pocket.

In another corner of the room, there was another man watching Faye. Damon Caruso was the local barista, and a good friend of Faye. He was making coffees for those here today, but on his mind first and foremost was Faye herself. He fancied her, and for the past several years, he'd been looking for a way to ask her out. He'd written note after note, poem after poem, all in an effort to win her over. His unread poems weren't always in vain, as he'd managed a few commendations from a local writers guild. He wasn't the next Edgar Allen Poe, but the prize money funded the stationery needed to write future unsent poetry to Faye.

However, they were good friends, and the threat of sacrificing that was a touch too much for Damon. His feelings for her were strong, but their friendship was stronger. She confided in him, he listened. He was a rock in her life when she needed a friend. Growing up, she had a tough family life and Damon was often the friend she went to.

This trust created an awkward dynamic. Their friendship was strong and asking her out could totally dissolve it. Remembering this, he slid his note back down into his pocket. Despite spending hours geeing himself up, he decided against it, as he'd done many times prior.

'One day,' he murmured.

Council Meeting

With the spectre of her crimes looming over the Urban Foraging community, Jim and Shelly had called an urgent meeting with the Council of Foragers to discuss the Faye situation. Converging at the top-secret location on Quandong Avenue in a prominent lime-coloured building, Jim had frantically written an emergency email at 1 am. The very foundations that Urban Foraging were built on were crumbling, all due to one young woman with a flagrant disregard for her confrere.

Jim greeted the councillors as they sat down and started masticating the complimentary jam scones. 'Thanks for meeting with us on such short notice.' With a PowerPoint presentation lined up and a point n' clicker in hand, he began, 'I've called everyone here to address a pressing issue arising in our quaint little community.'

'To put it bluntly,' Shelly interjected, sipping her Devonshire tea, 'something is rotten in the state of Tumut.'

'Damn straight,' Jim quipped, before emphatically clicking his point n' clicker. Unfortunately, he faced immediate technical difficulties: his clicker wasn't working. 'Blimey.'

As he tried to fix it, his fellow council of foragers waited …

And waited. And waited. With Jim's technological ineptitude being a frequent disruptor of many meetings, this began taking a while.

The council was small, just five members on the board inclusive of Jim and Shelly. There was Edna, the 77-year-old forager with a case of oncoming dementia, the burly town councillor and toy train set operator Derrick Dan Dan, and elderly Japanese metal detectorist Kenichi Kamataro.

Despite the reverence for regulations that Jim and Shelly displayed, these people didn't really care about these rules, not even the law-abiding Japanese man. They came for the Devonshire tea and the social occasion. They were lonely people who'd found a little community to share their passions with. Upholding a centuries-old code was secondary to finding a juicy mulberry tree in a seldom-visited enclave.

'This blimey … damn, ok I think I got it,' Jim grunted, before clicking onto the next slide, an overexposed picture of Faye foraging for mustard greens. 'I call your attention to this reckless young blow-in, Faye Friendly.'

'Not quite so friendly in my eyes,' Shelly quipped.

'Oh yes, young Faye,' Edna remarked, her withering memory coming back for a fleeting second. 'She drove me to my Sudoku night yesterday, a lovely young lass.'

'Speak for yourself,' Jim said.

'Nah, she won't speak for herself,' said Derrick Dan Dan, sitting upright in his chair and readjusting his train conductor's hat. 'She's an upstanding member of the community I'll have you know. She volunteers at the local food bank, does two shifts a week at the library, she regularly donates to her favourite charity. I won't hear anyone besmirching the lassie's name.'

'She's wonderful,' Kenichi remarked, mouth covered with cream as he was three scones deep into a box of 12. Despite usually maintaining a strict diet, his scone fix every second Saturday was his time to gorge himself. A slight bit of pudge peeked from underneath his shirt indicative of his sweet tooth.

'Well,' Jim moaned, disappointed by the indifference of his consiglieres, 'as the great poet Benoit Piccadilly once said, every Venus flytrap has a bite.'

'And every night has its dawn,' Shelly quipped, the two bouncing off each other like metal balls on a perpetual motion device. The reference may have been ill-placed, but the flytrap that Faye was setting was fooling many Tumut citizens who were just trying to get on with their lives and various affairs.

'Damn straight, but no, not damn straight, because the malingering shadow this young woman casts over our community won't cease.'

Shelly agreed, banging her hand against the desk. 'No, it won't.'

'Unless we strongly reprimand her for her mischievous actions.' At that moment, Jim emphatically clicked his clicker: the next slide showed Faye placing a handful of stinging nettles in the same bag as a whole bunch of Eucalyptus leaves.

Before he could explain this transgression, Kenichi quipped, 'I'll tell you something Jim, I hope you don't find my mastication of these scondiments mischievous, because I'm treating myself today.' Kenichi dug a little further into his big box of sweets, gorging on his fourth scone with his third different type of jam. He picked out a particularly creamy scone like it was stuck in thick cream, leaving behind an inexplicably sludgy mess within the box. Jam dripped from his pinkie finger, leaving stains over the withered old tablecloth with many holes and frays. This would usually infuriate Shelly, but the matter at hand prevented her from being more outraged than she usually would be.

Jim ignored Kenichi, clicking through his slides, each picture as damning as the last. 'This young woman has been doing it all. Mixing her stinging nettles in with her legumes, over-harvesting pheasant berries, and perhaps worst of all, she's been picking individual sumac leaves, leaving whole plants half-picked like a man hurriedly picking his nose in the office. Such transgressions threaten the million little fibres of our blanketed little community.'

'Uh, no,' Derrick interjected, licking the tips of his fingers to remove excess cream, 'it doesn't affect anything, mate. Sure, some of these practices are rookie mistakes, but I think with a bit of guidance, we—'

'Guidance?' Shelly interrupted, tea dribbling out of her mouth. 'Do you think someone like this can be guided? She's like a rabid wild Brumby, unbreakable.'

A second passed, then Derrick pontificated on that slightly erroneous simile. 'Mate, you can break a Brumby.'

Shelly shouted, 'I'll break you, you piece of …'

'Woah woah woah woah woah,' Jim said, getting in between the two foragers. 'See what this indecorous vagabond is doing to us?'

'Sending us mad,' Shelly admitted, breaking from her fury and sitting back down. Tensions were flaring; the foraging community faced a threat greater than most. This sort of bubbling ill feeling had been explained by the forefathers of foraging; forewarnings left throughout the great literature such as *To Pick a Purslane?* or *The Ground Elderberries of the Higher Realm*. A once reputable pastime was devolving into a vanity project for the worst society had to offer; Jim and Shelly had enough.

'See what this fiend has done to us?' Jim asked the group, head down as he pressed his knuckle into the table below.

'I don't know, she's a friend to me,' said Kenichi, licking jam off his chops, 'much like this subtle marmalade, yummo!'

'No friend to us, no friend to Tumut, no friend to the gosh darn world,' Shelly said, each point met with a harder fist-slam, leaving a small indent in the less-than-sturdy old table they'd been gathered around.

With hands pressed together and a sombre look on his jowly face, Jim warned, 'If she refuses to take our codes and practices seriously, then I can't be held accountable for the actions I deem necessary to take.'

Derrick Dan Dan, slowly backing away from the desk, made the inquiry one would make after such bizarre ramblings. 'Guys, is everything ok? Are all your matters in order?'

Shelly answered, rather stoically, 'We're taking matters into our own hands, as we've done before.' And on that point, the two foragers stormed out of the room. The three less-than-dedicated roamers of the urban jungle were left with nothing but regret, tension, and the scones that Kenichi hadn't gotten to. This humble profession had been reduced to a joke, a comedy show for everyone to laugh at …

Urban Foraging was a serious practice to be respected and revered.

To Pick a Purslane?

Knock Knock Knock. Faye's knocking on Ivana Zrebrenica's door reverberated down the main street of Adelong. Nestled in a valley near Tumut, Adelong was more a graveyard than a town. Awashed in a sea of elderly folks with strollers and walkers, the town didn't look like it used to. A once thriving community, the people of Adelong had grown quite weary. Unkempt and unwashed, the town's streets paralleled the grooming habits of these aging Adelongians with urban decay and dismay evident on the faded stop signs and shopfronts. Most of the stores in this town had been abandoned for decades. If it weren't for a small butchery, florist, fishmonger and fruit market, the Adelongian faithful would be forced to make the perilous trip to Tumut, potentially cataclysmic considering the sheer amount of wrecked cars left abandoned near the town.

This lack of upkeep left them susceptible to the agenda-driven ideologues of the Submergist Movement. On every street corner, placards, billboards and flyers were plastered on like a chipped porcelain tile in a poorly kept rental. The town had become overrun with 'SUBMERGE' signs, explaining the 97 percent support for the movement within Adelong. It was considered a town full of gullible people, where climate denialism bled into neighbourly disputes over whether it was appropriate to mow the patch of your neighbour's lawn that meets the fence.

A notable example of this gullibility was when mayor Niall Smythe sued then-Tumut mayor Dickhead Derrigan for claiming the word 'gullible' was written on the roof of the local fish and fruit market *The Fishy Cherry*. After a protracted legal battle, Niall was defeated in court and forced to admit that he was duped by his mayoral counterpart.

It was the butt of many jokes within the Snowy Valleys, mainly due to the strangely enlarged arses of its male population. To get into the perplexities of Adelong required a book, and this isn't the one for such a daunting task.

The soft voice of Ivana called out, 'Come in my dear.'

Faye entered the house, always amazed by Ivana's massive collection of Green Bottles. Glass or plastic, biodegradable or biohazardous, Ivana's house was possibly the largest gathering of Green Bottles in the southern hemisphere, something she'd been begging to get officially recognised for years. Letter after letter, phone call after phone call, Ivana had been desperate to get validation for her diligent work of maintaining this collection. The most she'd ever received was a single letter, telling her to, quote, 'Fuck off'.

Faye took her seat on the living room couch and waited for the coffee that Ivana was inevitably making. She marvelled at the aforementioned bottles; strategically placed LED lights oscillating through each, creating a surreal effect within this dimly lit room. To the layman passing through, Ivana's collection was a bit weird for a genteel Croatian lady to possess. However, for the learned members of the Greater Snowy Valleys, this was a delicately crafted masterpiece by a gifted auteur. If one of these 1,079 Green Bottles were to accidentally fall, you would see a cultural tragedy not seen since the destruction of the tetrapylon monuments in Palmyra.

Ivana came racing out with her coffee. She wore her traditional red marama head scarf with grey sweatpants, an attire she seemingly never stopped wearing. 'Young Faye, my girl, tell me what you've been up to?'

Ivana handed the indescribably strong coffee to Faye, which she politely sipped. Ivana often claimed that this was an authentic brew sourced straight from her home village of Pag. However, due to its revolting taste and the suspicious amount of International Roast tins strewn throughout her house, the authenticity of these claims was debatable.

'Well Ivana, where do I start?' Faye sipped her coffee. 'I've been volunteering for a few charities around the place. Uh … I've been looking into a career in botany through my university studies. I'm saving up for a house, and yeah, that's about it.' Faye smiled, her smile growing wider at the sight of Ivana's excited eyes. Ivana was so proud of Faye and was genuinely pumped to see her do well.

'Wonderful, my girl.' Ivana picked up a book on her table about the famed professional pie-eater Ken Kensford, aimlessly flicking through it. 'It sounds like you've been taking the bull by the horns as they say.'

'I've even taken up a bit of Urban Foraging in my downtime, just to learn about plants and—'

'Hold on girly!' Ivana interrupted, her demeanour completely changing into something frantic and mortified. 'Did you say that you were taking up Urban Foraging, my girl?'

'Yeah Ivana, a little bit, when and where I can really.'

Ivana chucked away her book before springing to her feet and racing towards her bookshelf, looking for something more pertinent to the situation.

'Are you at all aware of the sordid history of this practice my dear?' Ivana had a heaviness in her breath, as if her life were in danger. She scoured her bookshelf, clearly looking for something in particular.

She picked out a picture of a man in a mayoral garb covered in poison ivy and the flaxen hair of the lass by his side. She fixated on one particular feature buttoned onto the mayor's jacket, before throwing it away.

Faye looked on, a little concerned that Ivana's mental state had taken this erratic changing of tune. Faye peered over to the discarded book, noticing another picture from that book; that same mayoral character low-blowing a man who looked awfully similar to the man she'd seen watching her.

'That's it, girl,' Ivana said, slightly exasperated, '*To Pick A Purslane?* is the seminal work within Urban Foraging lore, perhaps more so than Dilanthanaweera Diplendriademico's *Daisies for Delirium*, a work so piercing that most who read it finish with several puncture marks in their abdomen.' Ivana sculled her coffee and proclaimed, 'Girl, this book explains the great evils that lie on the path you've embarked on.' Ivana extended the book out to Faye, who promptly took it and began to peruse through the passages.

This only furthered questions vis-à-vis the mental state of Ivana. The whole book was filled to the brim with cryptic poetry; with admittedly stunning landscape photography to accompany it. The famed Benoit Piccadilly knew his way around the ISO function, but his ability to write accessible stanzas was severely hindered by his severe dyslexia and creative disagreements with translator Dickolas Destitute, which bled over into his work. Ever a petty man, Dickolas used Benoit's broken command of the English language as an excuse to air some particularly dirty laundry about the famed writer. It served as a blessing in disguise, however, as Benoit had been looking for an excuse to divorce his darling wife Dottie.

As Faye struggled to decrypt these abstruse verses, Ivana politely asked, 'Is it all making sense to you, girl?'

'Ivana dear, with all due respect, I don't really get what he's trying to say.'

'Bullshit, girl, read a little deeper.' With a sigh, Faye tried reading one of these poems aloud.

'A Brush With Apostasy, A Canola Covered Fantasy

A Date with Destiny, a Rose-Coloured Bed …

Faye's gaze shifted away from the book, locking with Ivana's deep-blue eyes.

'Ivana, I don't mean to be rude, but this sounds a bit like erotica.'

'BULLSHIT, GIRL.' Ivana leapt back to her feet. 'This is about the harrowing tale of how the Snowy Valleys were founded, and how those within the Urban Foraging business tried to destroy society itself.'

'It's not sexual?' Faye inquired.

'Mind out of the gutter girl, read it!' Faye kept her gaze on Ivana for a second, before putting her eyes back down on the book.

She flicked back to a new page, continuing,

'A Cannibalistic Dalliance …'

Faye's eyes shot back to Ivana, who eagerly awaited the next line. 'An ad, an ad for Allianz?'

'That's not the line, girl!'

'I know, I'm talking about this?' Faye held up a book to show an ad for the insurance company. The book was littered with many such ads, more than even your stock standard edition of *K-Zone*. The literature on Urban Foraging wasn't always destined for the bestsellers list, so many authors had to make their moolah using quirky and innovative methods. Advertising was one such example. A method that Ivana tried to wave off.

'Girl, you worry too much, just keep reading.'

'Keep reading this erotica?'

'This masterpiece of a cautionary tale.'

Faye wasn't convinced. 'Ivana, are you sure this isn't erotica?'

'Girl, would I sully your eyes with degenerate filth?' Ivana smiled, trying to urge Faye to read on. This was a gripping piece of art for Ivana, but for Faye, this was an examination of the severely ill-adjusted psyche of writer Benoit Piccadilly, as well as a detailed description of the many fetishes of the man himself. Retrospectively, it made sense that the first edition came with a free ball gag and nipple clamps, many of which are now collectors' items stored within Snowy Valley pawn and porn shops.

Faye cleared her throat before flicking to the next page. Along with the smut, she continued,

> *'Cum into my Eye, The Ball Gag I wear.*
>
> *Spit On My Face, Tear at my hair.'*

'Yeah girl, that's him talking about his struggles with political corruption, especially with those landfarin' layabouts in Tumut.'

Less than impressed, Faye slammed the book shut and placed it on the table. Graphic depictions of various BDSM methods were not going to convince Faye that Urban Foraging was a bit suss, but it may keep her away from the various writers who still loiter around the Snowy Valleys.

'No offence, Ivana, but I'm not here to read one's erotic fantasies, I've got work to do.' Faye walked out of the house, leaving Ivana to her own devices, several of which could be heard vibrating from a nearby bedroom.

'You haven't even read *The Torrid Tryst of Tumut*, a defining moment of the town's legacy. Come back, girl!'

Ivana was left alone, Faye free to continue foraging. Ivana became enraptured with dread, fearing that Faye could be walking into trouble. This was a world where greed influenced governance, where sloth and sin synergise. Where land shills refuse to grow gills. It wasn't for those looking for a quick Sunday thrill.

For Faye, however, she figured she wasn't going to learn anything useful from *The Torrid Tryst of Tumut*. Unless she were to start an interesting sex life.

A Bottlebrush with the Law

For local police officer Harris Headingly, the monotonous hum of the air conditioner annoyed him ever so slightly. He grunted as he dropped the temperature down a couple of degrees, hoping that'd do the trick. Added with the background ambiance of *Honey, We're Killing the Kids* on the tele, this was the most lively this little office had been for a while. In a town of high moral order and civil obedience, being a police officer was about as listless as watching seagulls flocking on a secluded beach in France. No one had been arrested for months, no felons caught, and peace seldom disturbed; despite the best efforts of Submergist activists. The unacknowledged reality of his life weighed heavy on his mind; he was a cop in name only. He served more as a school speaker, a trusted voice to warn kids of the dangers of marijuana or jaywalking.

However, with a rotten stench festering within the town of Tumut – as well as the police station fridge – two wayward wayfarers were determined to give him something to do. Almost knocking the rickety old door off its hinges, Jim and Shelly blustered into the station like a paper bag caught in the wind. It was an entrance dramatic enough to make Harris spill a little bit of tea, the resulting stains the first that'd seeped into his uniform in a long time.

With a certain amount of zhuzh, Jim greeted the stultified sergeant. 'Officer Headingly, my dearest compatriot.'

'An upstanding public servant,' Shelly added. 'We're here to inform you of a most disturbing crime.' Shelly made a dry gurgling sound as if she were about to spit out some imaginary mouthwash.

'A disrobing of the silence, a breaker of the peace,' Jim volleyed, accompanied by a dramatic opening of his trench coat revealing his garish attire to the stupefied sergeant.

'Involving a reckless young woman with a penchant for malfeace.'

These accusations were a bit much for Headingly, who'd been lazily filling out the sudoku section in *The Quinty Sentiment*. Despite being a man with nothing to do, he often found a way to keep himself occupied. Whether listening to The Smiths or solving a Rubik's cube, Headingly was never one to find himself twiddling his thumbs. Panic on the streets of Tumut was something he needn't be concerned about.

This had to be a pretty serious crime to awaken him from his investigatory slumber. 'What is it?' he asked. His clear disinterest didn't register with Jim, who proceeded to inform him of these most malicious crimes.

'Faye Friendly.'

'Not so friendly,' Shelly snarled, nose flaring in disgust from hearing Faye's name.

'Has been sullying the upstanding reputation of Urban Foraging in Tumut.'

'And the broader Snowy Valleys for that manner.'

'With her ill-gotten gains.'

'It's driving us insane!'

The two foragers were already starting to get under the skin of Harris Headingly. With a clicking of his pen and a rolling of his eyes, he sat upright to file his report. Harris didn't really know where to start. He wasn't well versed on forager law, lore, or much else by his own admission. He was a simple man who liked fixing his 30-year-old beat-up Holden Commodore. He enjoyed the occasional game of lawn bowls with his old mates, and a glass of plonk with his darling wife, Darlene. These various hobbies left him little space to study the often-fraught history of Urban Foraging.

He turned to the second page of his barely used notebook covered in spiderwebs and a years-old ink blotch. Clearing his throat, he asked his first question. 'So guys, what crimes has this Faye Friendly committed?' Without a moment's hesitation, Jim whipped out a scroll that unfurled to the ground; about two meters of the scroll resting on the creaky wooden floor for the ants to gnaw on.

Jim cleared the phlegm in his oesophagus. 'Item number one: Faye Friendly has repeatedly harvested the prickly pear out of season.'

'A prick move, from this prickly pair of legs.'

'Item number two.'

'It takes two to tango.'

'She has been caught over-harvesting her mustard greens.'

'That's fairly obscene.'

'It'll put knots in ya spleen!'

Harris was dumbfounded by these two. How can two individuals who'd spent their time wandering in nature feel like they need to touch grass? Despite having an abundance of resources freed up, Harris felt this to be a total waste of time. He crossed his arms and leaned back.

Nevertheless, Jim continued. 'Item number three.'

'We have a crowd now.'

'No, you don't,' Harris interjected, already having enough of this masturbatory exercise. 'Police resources should be allocated to important things, like neighbourhood security and peacekeeping. Quite frankly … I don't see how this should be worthy of my time.'

Jim and Shelly glared at Harris. They were tackling an existential threat to their community, beaten perhaps only by climate change. It seemed like the police weren't on their side for this one. After a minute of awkward silence, Jim decided to barrel ahead, hoping a few more transgressions could sway the surly policeman.

'As I was saying, Item number three.'

'Uno, dos, tres.'

'Faye Friendly has repeatedly harvested morning glory out of season.'

'What's her story?'

'That'll leave her guts gory!'

This was becoming a bit absurd for Harris, who let out an audible groan. The droning of these two had become physically painful, and Harris felt this like a steel knife.

'Item num—'

'Tumut Police Station isn't the forum to air your menial grievances, get out!' Harris signalled towards the door, which was slightly ajar and swinging like a rusty old gate in a gale-force wind. Jim and Shelly were peeved at this odious officer. A failure to act was a failure to govern, and this man's inaction meant the breakdown of common order.

'So you, as an ambassador of the law, are willing to let this problem fester?' Jim asked with a childish naivety Harris had only experienced through a red-headed kid asking if he'd used his gun before.

'To pester and jester?'

'I. Don't. Care,' said Harris, picking up his Sudoku puzzle. 'Good day, freaks.' Harris continued along his merry way down a crossword, a 6 down, two across regression back into banality. He'd experienced many unserious complaints before. These included a local fisherman wanting Harris to investigate if a giant yabby had burrowed inside the Tumut River. Local mothers wanting a welfare cheque for a son who'd only left the house one hour earlier. Even aggrieved Submergist activists had reached out, wanting Harris to initiate a royal commission into whether current Mayor Phuck Whitton was a Maoist double agent looking to bring Tumut under land-based CCP rule. Despite this, none of these complaints annoyed the surly sergeant more than Jim and Shelly's; an encounter that truly made him question his career choices.

Needless to say, Jim and Shelly were miffed by such dedication to inaction. With a serious tone, Shelly whispered, 'You leave us no choice.'

She proceeded to open her overcoat, revealing a fanny-pack underneath. The contents of the bumbag weren't the only shrubbery growing wild in these areas, and it was far from being the deadliest.

However, it was still serious, and such a threat was enough to pull Harris away from his sudoku puzzle. With a stiffened posture, he sternly warned the duo.

'I am obliged to warn you, any act of vigilantism will be met with a swift response.' Tensions festered for a second, as both parties were caught in a standoff. The twitching of the hands and the beating of hearts were the only things moving in that room. This was a standoff not indicative of the usually jovial mood of the town, even the town's various Irish travellers and Submergist activists opted for sternly worded letters as opposed to an old-fashioned donnybrook.

Sergeant Headingly – realising where this was leading – reached for his handcuffs, a common bluff he used to warn people against malfeasance. Before he could feel the cold, comforting aluminium around his fingers, his face was met with a strong, sharp stinging sensation.

'Oh my god, what the …'

'Vigilante justice, my friend,' Jim explained as Shelly closed up her fanny-pack. Harris fell to the ground, writhing in pain. It felt like a thousand hot needles had rained down over him, rendering him a bit cooked. In reality, he was covered by a net, which had been lined with stinging nettle and Patterson's Curse.

A seldom used device, Shelly's Cursed Nettle was originally designed to fend off nefarious travellers; jaundiced Jacobites looking to pillage their plunder. Its use on Sergeant Headingly may not have been fit for purpose, but it was a way to protect her booty from imminent seizure.

Shelly wasted no time, grabbing out a roll of string twine and subduing the sergeant. A line across the mouth rendered him silent, a roll over the eyes meant justice was blind. As Harris felt the strong twine clamp his wrists, he knew that the tools of justice had been severely hampered.

'Quick Shelly, trap him inside.'

Shelly pulled herself away from the officer, returning to her lover wearing a proud smirk. She briefly glanced over her shoulder, admiring her handiwork. With a nod, the two foragers raced out of the station, slamming shut the door behind them. Thinking quickly, Jim reached into his tote bag and pulled out his own trusty bundle of twine. With the speed and accuracy few possessed or cared to learn, he wrapped the twine around the door handle, trapping Headingly inside. The muffled screams of Harris rung hollow; he was a prisoner of his own domain.

As Jim finished twining, he turned to Shelly. It was a look of steely determination, as if he knew what perilous paths lay ahead.

'Shelly.'

'Jim.'

'We're outlaws now.'

'Vigilantes of Justice.'

'Wielding the weapons of war.'

'Our weapons used, like an old whore.' Jim and Shelly shared an earthy kiss that tasted of unwashed mushrooms and tree sap. Their path was now evident. If their fellow councilpersons weren't of use, and their local police department refused to investigate Faye's malfeasance, they were now tasked with taking matters into their own hands.

Vigilantes

'Let the communist curl up and die,

It's fairly bizarre, how they love the tsar,

that Dastardly Bastard from Zanzibar'

Through the rustic laneways of Tumut, a small yet vocal minority of Pro-Submergist partisans marched. With placards held aloft, they railed against the council's seventh rejection of their proposition. Withered down by the stresses of land-faring life, they'd tirelessly advocated for the Snowy Valleys to be sunken into the abyss. No longer shall they breathe the dry air of the relentless Riverina summer, instead they sought to scour the seas; and live a life of ease!

Anti-Submergist groups argued that it was a rather silly idea to sink an entire town underwater.

Pro-Submergist activists argued that opposition to their plan was a Maoist plot orchestrated by both Callum the Tsar from Zanzibar and Alan Kerzog from Kritschnia to implement communism with land-faring characteristics. Despite a lack of evidence to these claims and the differing political ideologies of their bogeymen, these protesters had a certain tenacity to their belief. If their rambling 12-hour filibusters at local council meetings were any indicator, this could drag on for a while.

This social unrest provided ample backdrop for Jim and Shelly to become vigilantes. They watched these protests from a nearby parklet, periscopes peering at the pickets from afar. They saw a town teetering towards anarchy, and only those operating outside normal jurisprudence could restore any sort of normalcy.

'Civil unrest,' Jim opined.

'Our biggest test,' Shelly replied. The protesters' chants echoed from afar, distracting the town and allowing the two to begin implementing their plan. Jim handed Shelly a bundle of posters and placards.

'My love.'

'Mine all mine.'

'Let's get to it, shall we?'

'We shall …'

With a nod of the hand and a light peck on the lips, the foragers sent each other on their way. With the distinct sound of yodelling from local buskers ringing through the streets, they began spreading awareness, along with some errant head lice. They hung these posters in cafés, in bars, on cars, furled up into cigars. Flyers were forced upon passers-by, and promptly thrown away. These urgent forewarnings quickly became recycled trash, soon to be repurposed into posters and flyers on more pertinent concerns within the broader Snowy Valley.

Once they were out of posters, they began their more malevolent plan. With a scout's handbook in hand, they began laying traps in various foraging hotspots around Tumut. Glue traps were first, followed by the figure-four deadfall. From there, the traps became more and more deadly. A punji stick pit was placed at Stony Creek, a place where Faye frequently picnicked with friends. If she were to sit in her usual spot, then this well-laid plan could ensure a shitty end to a rather splendid outing.

After a few more hours of trap-setting and awareness-raising, the two reconvened at their foresty hidey-hole. It was hard yakka, the most strenuous days' work in many years for the unemployed couple. Sweat had been poured, blisters and sores. They'd felt accomplished, in their own perverse way.

'It's a dirty job.'

'But somebody's gotta do it Jimothy.' The two hugged. Earthworms, lice and blowflies took this moment to transfer between hosts; the organisms pleased to escape the confines that were the unwashed crevasses of each forager. They looked over the town from a vantage point, a single flare rising from a faraway street suggesting a bit of trouble but not too much to warrant concern. This was the path they'd chosen, outside the confines of common law. They may not be comfortable with this fact, but they had to adapt as if they were forced to sleep on barbed wire to save their family.

Looking at his last scroll of Faye, Jim spat on it. The thick phlegm rolled down the cheek of Faye. No tears for the wicked, only spit from the nitid and sunbathed.

'I really don't like her, hun.'

'I despise her.' Shelly, too, spat on the photo of Faye. Jim began ripping apart the scroll, Shelly fishing a pair of matches out of her tote bag. The fire in their eyes was about to transfer onto the page, their rage boiling like a pot on the stove.

However, before they could set fire to Faye, a tiny little voice rang out from the forest behind them.

'Excuse me, feller!'

The two swung around to see a short, feisty creature. With a crown on its head, it strutted towards them like royalty despite no other evidence of royal title. The fabled figure of folklore looked up at the foragers with a hand up, and their second hand out.

'Do ya mind tellin' me where the Golden Clover of Tumut is?'

In front of them was Slevin the Leprechaun; a persistent pest to the good people of Tumut and someone that Jim never wished to encounter. Like a leech to the skin, Slevin was something you needed to get rid of quickly, with much more vinegar than it usually took to kill the pesky skull suckers.

'Bugger off,' Jim grunted, putting a piece of morning glory between his teeth.

'Ya folkloric freak.'

'Ya mythical geek.'

Jim hocked a golly to the side. 'I prefer the fairies.'

Slevin was used to gaining a harsh reception, his presence often as welcome as an STD at an orgy. Their origins were unknown to the people of Tumut. He just showed up at a local cockfighting ring to fight prized rooster *Wandering Dasher*, an Australorp owned by disreputable local 'journalist' Former Luland. Upon beating the cocksure cock, he proceeded to bite the heel of Luland repeatedly, which led to a 20-minute knockdown, drag-out brawl. After that battle, he lingered around like a Cranberries song on repeat, annoying the Tumut faithful with his begging, stealing and freewheeling.

The Leprechaun was initially hurt by Jim's comments and proceeded to walk away. However, as he looked down to his left, he saw the torn-up photo of Faye Friendly. Her deep blue eyes were alluring, like she was a succubus drawing him into her lair to be devoured. Slevin had been seduced by many succubi back in his day. However, since they had no soul, they couldn't devour them like their usual victims. They was just left to whimper away, going about their day.

They turned back towards the couple, with a most enticing question. 'Fellers, you trying to capture Faye not-so-Friendly?' The foragers stop in their tracks, their heads slowly turning towards the lecherous leper.

'Perhaps,' Jim said, a single eyebrow raised into an almost perfect arch, reminiscent of the *Arch de Triomphe* if it was infested with micro-organisms and a stray spiderweb.

'What's it to you?' said Shelly, raising an eyebrow. Notorious for his mischievous ways, Slevin was not to be trusted in the eyes of Tumutians. Shelly knew this had a catch. 'Why do you take interest in our apprehension of Faye, youngster?'

The Leprechaun corrected Shelly – 'Lassie, I'm a thousand years old.' – before wiping his coat and explaining. 'I know a few fellers looking to give favours, aye?'

'Like what favours?' Jim asked.

Shelly wasn't too impressed with Jim for taking this leper seriously. A man with ringworm visible from their rolled-up sleeves, she suspected this to be a ploy to steal their booty or pickpocket their plunder.

She glared at Jim, who didn't really see what she was seeing.

'Shelly, my love. We owe it to this youngster to hear him out.'

'I'm not young, I'm older than the Irish potato famine, feller. Me daddy fought Oliver Cromwell. Show some respect for your seniors.'

'Well … You haven't aged, so take it as a compliment.' Jim proceeded to condescendingly lean down. 'What are you offering?'

Slevin kicked Jim in the shin, knocking him down. He groaned in pain like a man being tortured, apropos considering Slevin's presence was akin to waterboarding on a Sunday afternoon.

'Agh, you damned—'

Slevin interrupted Jim as he seethed in pain. 'Well, firstly, the offer will only stand if you don't lean down to me, I'm not some Culchie to look down upon.'

'Fine,' Jim snapped, lifting up his pant leg. A bruise was forming.

Slevin showed no concern and proceeded forth. 'Good. I help ye apprehend this cursed wench, and in return, you help me and the fellers find the Golden Clover.'

Shelly scoffed at this offer and Slevin was none-too impressed by her response. 'C'mon fellers, I need this. If anyone knew where it would be, it'll be you, Mr Jimothy.'

Jimothy shot Slevin a look of interest.

The Golden Clover was an urban legend around Tumut; a tale too preposterous to believe. As legend goes, in 1914 Mayor Finnlaigh Cumlach was caught in courtship with the Queen of Luxembourg. Upon hearing reports that Finnlaigh had sired her child, the King of Luxembourg ordered 200 men to travel to Australia to capture or kill Finnlaigh. Sensing danger, he reportedly buried himself – along with his vast wealth and 50 years' worth of spam and beans – in a grave somewhere near Tumut, the grave only detectable by a solitary golden four-leaf clover to mark its location.

Many members of the Tumutian community had spent years combing through the Snowy's in search of his grave. However, nobody had ever found so much as a five-cent coin belonging to the long-vanished Finnlaigh. The mayor himself was never found, most figuring he'd gone the way of a jolly swagman camping by a billabong. Some even claimed the clover also possessed the ability to give its holder immortality and everlasting youth, the fact that it was reportedly in Finnlaigh's possession seemed a bit too silly.

'Sure, I'll tell you where it is,' Jim murmured. The desperation was palpable in his voice, as if he were willing to deal with the devil himself. Shelly's eyes widened.

'You don't have the clover that raises the dead,' said Shelly.

'From their dour flowerbeds!

'Risen like good bread.' Jimothy tried to shoot an unsubtle wink at Shelly, who took a minute to catch on. Foragers were discouraged from believing in urban legend so as to not get their hopes up. Jimothy was known for telling the odd tall tale, however, so this was par for the course.

He dug into his bag pocket and fished out an envelope, before handing it to Slevin. 'This will lead you to it.' With a look of glee, Slevin scanned the map for a second.

'Perfect! I'll get the fellers onto it,' Slevin said, before happily skipping away into the distance. A deal with the devil can cost you your soul, but a partnership with a disreputable feller like Slevin can cost a man his dignity.

Jim gingerly rose to his feet, shin still stinging. With a foot like Robbie Keane in his prime, Slevin had done a number on Jim's lazy bones. He rolled up his trouser legs to inspect the damage. A considerable bruise was forming, and if he weren't to act quickly it could get infected or cursed, depending on whether Slevin had worn the wrong type of clogs.

Grabbing some morning glory out of his pocket, he began rubbing down his sore shin. Shelly was bemused by this whole experience.

'Jimothy, what are you doing?'

'I'm tending to my injury.'

'No, well, that too.' She crouched down to his level, pointing to the morning glory crumpled up between his hand and shin. 'Morning glory is to be ingested, a stimulant to the mind.'

'To make the dumb blind.'

'Yes, and it's not meant to be a remedy for your auspicious ailments.'

Jim was in breach of Law 157 in the Urban Foragers Code: never treat a wound with morning glory, it'll leave your guts gory. Jim, someone who strove to uphold these laws to a tee, quickly realised his mistake and hastily swallowed the plant.

Shelly wasn't done there, and with an inquiring look on her face, asked Jim, 'Why did you strike a deal with the devil?'

Jim ummed and ahhed for a second. In Urban Foraging dictum, a Forager must get a deal in writing and hand shaken upon, to protect against the seizure of booty. In Jim's time of desperation, he'd neglected to do this; a misdemeanour that'd see a man with less power suitably chastened.

'Um …' he stammered on that point, looking around for answers. After a moment of silence, he stumbled upon an answer. Picking up a nearby mound of faecal matter, he ran his left hand through the muck, causing Shelly to stammer away in disgust. Smearing a little on his face, he began his hasty rationalisation.

'Shelly, sometimes, you have to break the law to enforce your jurisprudence.' Jim closed his eyes and started rubbing the dung on his eyelids. 'Sometimes, you have to get a little dirty in the quest to exercise said jurisprudence. It's a bit shitty, but you've gotta do what you gotta do.' Jim hopped to his feet, before walking past Shelly and retreating to his hidey-hole, a fallen tree stump nearby.

Shelly spent a minute trying her best not to vomit. Using poop as a camouflage was a disgusting turn of events, even for Jim. She loved his soiled garments and unkempt appearance. His fungus-flavoured kisses got the pheromones racing more than any Mills and Boon novel. However, this was a touch too much.

That didn't even account for her displeasure towards Slevin and Jim's unholy union. She wanted to keep the peace in this town, but was dealing with this leper a necessary evil? Or a path towards perdition? With a bundle of morning glory to chew on, she wandered towards the hidey-hole where Jim lay, ruminating upon that very philosophical quandary …

Bounty of Bloodthorn

With the late autumn chill descending, young Faye wandered through the streets. She'd spent these days partaking in quixotic adventures, marvelling at the autumn leaves and foraging around her town. Ever the effervescent young lass, Faye greeted many who walked by with a smile brighter than the leaves she marvelled. This sunny disposition made her a beloved figure within the broader Snowy Valleys, and her humility consolidated her status as one of the brightest flowers this town had sprouted.

Upon arriving at her favourite coffee and movie shop, *The Bean Flick*, she was greeted by a most peculiar sight. A WANTED poster – written on an old, weathered scroll with slightly burnt edges – hung high in the coffee shop window. It furled down to the ground, the bottom of the poster resting perilously close to some dog poop, slightly chewed and lightly soiled.

The sight of this poster was mystifying. Who made it? And who even cared enough to distribute it? She read through a few of the transgressions ... 88 in total. It listed many of her foraging faux pas, with a few of her broader moral failings also coming into question.

Wanting to investigate this, she entered *The Bean Flick* to ask about its display. This was a place she frequented; two coffees a day and the odd Marlon Brando picture for when she's feeling a bit adventurous. It was where her mates congregated and conversed, where she'd had her first kiss two years earlier. Surely, they'd have a good reason for this poster hanging on their window like a shiny Christmas mistletoe.

Upon entering the store, she was greeted by Damon Caruso, the similarly bubbly young lad with a passion for coffee and a crush on the young lass herself. The sparkle in his eye shined brighter than the sparkly piercing that sat burrowed in his ear like an emerald in a rock formation.

'The friendliest Faye in the Snowy's, a matcha with skim and a James Dean classic?'

'Uh ...' she replied, 'yeah, but also, what's with the poster?' Damon looked over to his right, noticing the unfamiliar display in the window. He knitted his brow, then shrugged.

'Um … it wasn't there when I got in, and I've been so busy with these coffees that I haven't paid much attention to the goings on around me.'

'Hmm …' These transgressions didn't seem like a big deal, to her or anyone within her proximity. Why was such an issue taken with her?

As Damon got to making her matcha, Faye began perusing through local lifestyle magazine *The Tumut Turnstyle*. She mindlessly flicked through the magazine for a few minutes, half-reading but also peering up in anticipation of her matcha. Her mind was elsewhere, however.

It was indicative of a much weirder phenomenon. Ever since she'd started foraging, things just didn't seem right. From this scroll to Ivana's strange behaviour, to the constant feeling that someone was watching her, Faye's foraging endeavours were met with strangeness. It made her wonder whether this was the right hobby for her, or if knitting would've been a better use of her downtime. It raised some rather philosophical questions, while also causing her to consider carrying a cheese knife for protection.

As she watched Damon pour milk ever so gently into her cup, he noticed her and shot back a polite smile. Damon had been pondering whether he should finally ask her out. He'd come close so many times, but as always, he just didn't have the courage to pull the pin. He was too scared of changing the dynamic of a perfectly good friendship. While it was nice that they hung out often and saw each other regularly, deep down he wanted a bit more. Faye was like an angel, his feelings for her resting heavy in his mind.

'Hey, Faye?' he said, almost involuntarily. His hands went clammy as he sprinkled cinnamon onto her coffee. She turned her head, her long eyelashes a key point of focus as he looked at her.

'I was wondering …' he began, slightly biting his tongue as the internal battle within was being waged. These seconds seemed so long … He looked down at the slight mole above her lip, a flourishing feature on her beautiful face. This was his moment.

But his moment was lost in an instant. Outside of the café, a strange yodelling echoed through the streets. It made the windows vibrate and nearby birds migrate. The catchy tune also caused a few locals to dance and clap along, entranced by such a strange, folkish melody.

Catching her attention like a lure in a pond full of cod, Faye peered out the window. Through a crowd of love-struck couples gyrating and hip-shaking, a homeless-looking man with a leather jacket and long, straggly hair stood stoically with a tusk horn. He was dressed in woven suspenders, a feathered fedora, clogs, and very short cotton shorts. A bizarre fellow if ever she'd seen one, this man had an air of danger around him.

His yodelling came to an abrupt halt. 'Miss Faye the not-so-Friendly.' The man omitted sputum into a portable spittoon he carried on his waistband, 'You have made several transgressions in your urban foraging endeavours, a list too long to expound upon.'

At this stage, Faye slowly wandered towards the door, almost in a trance. Was this man some sort of weird bounty hunter? An officer of the law? Was he here to cause harm? To sound the alarm?

Her initial suspicions would be confirmed mere moments later. 'Miss not-so-Friendly, I am here to collect your bounty; a chest of collard greens and several thousand dollars in booty. Prepared to be apprehended.' The man reached down for his tusk horn and began playing a deep, obtuse tune before pulling out twine zip ties. Whether this man had jurisprudence to apprehend her didn't matter. He was bringing her in.

Faye stood at the entrance of this café, mortified. The man marched slowly, yet deliberately, towards her. Was she about to be kidnapped? Could she be killed? Who hated her enough to do either of those things?

Thinking on his feet, Damon handed her the boiling-hot cup of matcha. The bounty hunter reached for his peashooter. She had to act.

With a hefty loft, Faye tossed the boiling matcha all over this bounty hunter, the scalding water scarring this pathetic prowler. He bundled over like wooden blocks in a Jenga castle. The sizzle on his skin was like fresh steak on a hot skillet; satisfying yet not something you'd want to experience for yourself.

The patrons of *The Bean Flick* were shocked. The bounty hunter writhed as Faye stood over him. Damon raced over to check on her. She stood over this prowler with a certain detachment, emptiness in her eyes. Her matcha may have gone to waste, but her freedom – and possibly her life – had been spared.

'Faye, darl, are you alright?' Damon looked into her eyes but she just looked on, blankly.

'Look, come inside, I'll make you a fresh matcha. Also, I need to ask you …'

'No,' she said bluntly, 'I've got an errand to run.' Faye walked over to this bounty hunter, who'd been writhing in pain for a good minute. She gave him a pitiful look, before walking away. This was another departure of character from Faye, usually the type that'd put a band-aid on a graze or administer CPR if necessary. Even despite this man's attempts to apprehend Faye, it was very unlike her not to help him.

Which made Damon very worried. Wanting to double-check on her, he caught up to her and asked, 'Are you sure you're ok?'

Faye lifted her gaze and grabbed Damon by the shoulders. 'Damon, I'm afraid I'm heading towards the most lethal tête-à-tête.'

On that bombshell, Faye walked away. She wore a steely look in her eyes and a newfound intensity. Sure, she got a bit competitive during the local community Futsal tournaments, but this was very different.

Damon was left to watch on … His eyes followed Faye as she faded through the streets of Tumut like an evanescent memory. Those who'd joined the bounty hunter in dance were now tending to him, trying to prevent him from swallowing his tongue as he convulsed on the cold gravel of Wynyard Street.

He wasn't the only one left watching Faye …

'Shelly, my love.'

'Jimothy.'

'I think we're heading towards a tête-à-tête.'

'A tit-for-tat …'

'Fancy that!'

Jim and Shelly emerged from behind a garbage bin in front of the local art shop, dressed in camouflage and covered in a barely camouflaging blueberry viscus. Gawking at Faye from afar, the two nodded at each other before trailing off into the distance. This was a relief to the art shop owner, Hansie Hansfried, who'd lost several customers over the past hour due to these leering lurches.

And a few paintbrushes too.

The Venus Flytrap

Dressed in their Sunday best, Jim and Shelly were garrisoned behind a log. These wayward wayfarers – ecumenical in their devotion to foraging – were tumbling towards a tête-à-tête. Having dealt with the devil and broken the law, they were now operating on the fringe of society. Deluded desperados, holistic hold-uppers, deliverers of vigilante justice; their path was perilous.

With Doug the Bounty Hunter neutralised and Slevin nowhere to be found, Jim and Shelly had now resorted to plan B. They'd fallen back to the outskirts of Tumut, barricaded deep inside 'Foragers Forest'. Their new plan was simple. With the tale of the Golden Clover attracting disreputable ravagers to the region, they'd figured that this could be Faye's ultimate machination. They knew the lure of the leaf could be lucrative, their best chance to ensnare this jezebel once and for all.

They'd booby-trapped the entire forest with an array of contraptions. With thick vines entwining with their ropes – coupled with a distinct smell of cheese – their maze of misery was perhaps the most well-prepared, yet ill-conceived plan to bring Faye to justice. These traps were quite barbaric too; designed to maim the measly marauders looking to rummage the foliage that grew wild-like hair under the undergarments of each forager.

With moss-covered crosses around their neck, they awaited her arrival. This wasn't just an affront to their hobby, it was a true act of disrespect to their very existence. Faye couldn't be allowed to run rampant on the local Bermuda Buttercup population. She had to be stopped. She sometimes wore black on the outside, but it was nowhere near as black as she made these foragers feel on the inside.

Pulling out their trusty periscope, Jim peered out from behind the log. He scoured the forest, hoping to catch a glimpse of the cursed wrench herself. He peered to the left, glanced to the right. Nobody appeared in his line of sight. The aromatic smell of wild sumac was enough to lasso the noses of many. However, Faye was absent.

A few hours had passed, and the couple were starting to get agitated. With ants having a nibble on their heels, they wanted something to happen soon, before they were turned into a bundle of lazy bones.

'Darling,' Jim said.

'Jimothy,' Shelly replied, flicking away a ladybug that'd flown onto her collar.

'Maybe she's not coming.'

'What?'

'Maybe she took the attempted claim of her bounty as a sign to skedaddle.'

Jim and Shelly ruminated on that point. The history of foraging in the region was speckled with conflict. While they'd been documented in many of Benoit Piccadilly's seminal works, these incidents often got lost within the erotic prose. The imagery of caressing lily pads on a crisp spring morning often overshadowed the depictions of violent donnybrooks or sketchy conmen. Furthermore, those pages would get vomited on by readers before they'd gotten a chance to read through.

Shelly tried to respond to that point, but she had nothing. 'Well ...'

In a rare moment of clarity, both pondered on whether they could really catch her. A woman of such reckless abandon was sure to be crafty. She could disappear into the heat of the night, and nobody would be none the wiser. This was a cause for concern.

'We need to find her,' Jim stated.

'Arrest her.'

'Try her in front of a jury of our peers.'

'Bring her to lady justice.'

'Make her say …'

'AAAAAAHHHHHHHH!' A voice screamed from nearby, echoing like a desperate call for help inside a long dark tunnel. The two foragers were startled, ducking behind their log and arming themselves with peashooters. A male voice continued to scream out, causing a conundrum for the two foragers.

'Do we save this man Jimmy?' Shelly asked, shaking in fright. A grey area in Forager lore, the act of rescue often caused great philosophical debate within the Forager community. Some argued that it was a noble deed to rescue a practitioner in peril, while others argued that a call for help had been used by no-goodniks to lure people into donnybrooks. No matter where you stood, the stray asking for help always ended up worse off, as they had to meet with and spend time with an Urban Forager.

'He's a lost cause,' said Jim, 'a rancid weed, needing to be pulled.'

'Have you no humanity, my darling Jimothy?'

'I only have humanity for those who can be salvaged. In the case of …'

'I can hear you Jimothy, you asshole!' The voice revealed itself to be Kenichi, the detectorist and fellow member of the Council of Foragers. Kenichi wasn't one to venture into these parts, so his sudden appearance was a little shocking. If he wasn't near a plate of scones, something would have gone horribly wrong.

Jim and Shelly cautiously ventured to Kenichi's location, checking from side to side, double and triple checking that this wasn't a trap. Despite a decades-old friendship with Kenichi, both recognised the pliable personality he possessed. He could be convinced the earth was flat in one conversation, and corrected to the earth being spherical in the very next. If anyone in the Council of Foragers could be programmed into an agent provocateur, it was Kenichi.

Wading through the shrubbery for a good couple of minutes, they eventually reached the ensnared detectorist. Thankfully, he hadn't sustained a serious injury. However, there was one pretty obvious conundrum he faced, as he greeted the two foragers in a very sticky situation.

'Jim, Shelly, I'm stuck. Baka baka baka!' He exclaimed, trying to yank his metal detector out of a very specific place. Shelly looked down at the ground and immediately recognised what was going on.

'I'm afraid our good friend Kenichi …'

'The boy from Sendai.'

'… is stuck in one of our cunning traps.'

'Crap.' Kenichi had walked straight into a glue trap, one of several set by Shelly. Partially camouflaged through the wash of autumn leaves, Kenichi had followed the frantic beeping all the way to this spot, becoming seized in a most lethal glue trap. With booty potentially right under his feet, this was a peculiar predicament the elderly detectorist found himself in. Someone who was as deprived of booty as Kenichi had to take it where he could get it, no matter the circumstances.

He pleaded, trying to yank the metal detector from the industrial-strength glue. 'Help me, Jimothy?'

Shelly had used the good stuff, and prying Kenichi from the adhesive abyss could take a considerable amount of manpower. Beyond his metal detector being rendered useless, Kenichi had errantly taken one step into this trap, and he had gotten his left foot stuck in this abhorrent quagmire.

For the next few minutes, Jim tried a few different methods of freeing Kenichi. He tried yanking him out by his arms, applying some mistletoe berry to the foot, even going as far as pouring a little bit of hot water from his thermal jug. None of these things worked much to Jim's chagrin.

'Kenichi.'

'Our boy from Sendai.'

"I don't know what to do?' Jim said with a hand on Kenichi's shoulder in a conciliatory fashion. Kenichi in his misery sat down. This only made matters worse, as he planted his arse straight into the adhesive abyss. It took a second to register, but as he attempted to stroke his fundament, he realised that this made matters worse.

'Oh no, baka baka baka.'

'Bakna indeed,' Jim added, not the most helpful comment in this situation. Shelly was less than impressed with how everything was turning out.

'This wasn't our most well-thought-out plan, Jimothy.'

Jim spun around, angered by the pessimism of his darling wife Shelly. 'Don't think like that, Shelly.' He then grabbed her by the shoulders. 'This will work out, we will catch this derelict, and we will thoroughly reprimand her for her actions. Kenichi is a bit of a hopeless wanderer, there's very little chance anyone else will be ...' Jim looked at Kenichi, before drawing Shelly closer, '... bakna enough to fall for this.'

There was a brief silence ...

'Ah fuck, I've done it this time!' A voice rang out from somewhere behind them. Jim and Shelly turned around, and wouldn't you know who won the pony, another poor soul had become entrapped. Like Kenichi, this was a man very familiar to these two foragers.

Hanging by his ankle, local muckraking journalist Former Luland was swinging like an uncoordinated punch in the face. His pockets were overturned, below him a whole spring of wild thyme had dropped from his pockets. He looked bloodied and bruised as if he had nothing to lose.

'Mr Luland, bearer of good tidings.'

'G'day?' Luland said, drool running down his face. 'This is quite the peculiar predicament I've found myself in.'

'Why are you out in these parts?' Shelly inquired, looking down at the springs of wild thyme. 'Why do you have wild thyme? 'Tis not the season, you know?'

'I do know ...' Former started to say before breaking out into a particularly hoarse cough, phlegm dripping down his face like sap off a tree. 'But times are tough, and when *The Quinty Sentiment* asks me to cover stories beyond illegal cockfighting, you've got to venture into these murky enclaves to find a yarn.'

'I quite like your cockfighting coverage,' Jimothy quipped.

'Well, only you apparently.' Former spat out some viscus from his mouth. 'Apparently, it's "not real sport". Damn Steph Muir, telling me to cover "real" sport. Who else is going to cover Peruvian Cage Fighting and Professional Pie-Eating with the journalistic rigmarole that I do, gosh?' With the entrapment of this muckraking journalist, the error of their ways was a little more apparent.

'Jimothy, this isn't going to work.'

'It will,' Jim said, but before he could go on, the dropped thyme caught his eye. He dropped to his knees, inspecting the herb. It was still young, yet to fully bloom. An infraction like this could see you get a serious $20 fine or worse, permanent banishment from the world of Foraging.

However, Jim wasn't looking to exercise jurisprudence on the man.

'Today is your lucky day, Luland, I'll allow it.'

Shelly's eyes grew wide like the early morning sun. This roving roustabout had just committed an infraction as bad as any of Faye's misdemeanours, and Jimothy was letting this slide? Something was beginning to come over Jim. His regard for the law since turning to vigilantism was waning. It was a different Jim, not the fun-spirited law enforcer she'd fallen in love with. He was losing the thoroughness that she found so hot; Jimothy was slipping.

'Babe, this man is a crim.'

'Not the right type of crim.'

'Are you dim?'

'For what it's worth,' Former interjected, 'the smell coming from ya gob, boy that's grim, gosh!'

Shelly didn't care for Former's interjection, kicking him in the chin and knocking him out. Jim was shocked by this turn, quickly attending to Former as blood and phlegm poured from his face, the blood flowing apocalyptic to the small ant colony underneath him.

'Shelly, this man could've brought our story to life?'

'Have you read his articles?'

'Yeah.'

'The only thing he's bringing to life is his graphic depictions of rooster death.'

'Well …' Jim didn't have a retort, and he was starting to get a little bit annoyed at Shelly. He felt that she wasn't as interested in catching this societal scourge. Her trepidation towards Slevin, her assault of Former Luland. Shelly wasn't on the same train he was on. Maybe not even on the same line.

'Ah fuck, goddamn fucking fuck,' another voice rang out, this time it was that of an elderly female. Certainly not Faye. Jim and Shelly gave each other deathly glares.

'Look, Shell.'

'I'm looking Jimothy.'

'Maybe this is just fate.'

'Elaborate.'

'Maybe the lure of the cloverleaf will work. It's obviously luring these intrepid travellers. Perhaps Faye is on her way, and we can finally try her in front of a jury of her peers. Even if they are hanging upside down from trees.'

Shelly wasn't having it. 'Jimothy, I don't know if you're fully with it, darling.' Shelly proceeded to pick Former up by the scruff of his neck, 'You're letting ostentatious offenders …'

'Please help me, I'm stuck,' the elderly lady called out. Unfortunately, Shelly ignored her pleas for help, continuing her diatribe.

'… and delinquent derelicts get away from crimes. You're dealing with the devil.'

'I think Slevin is quite the pleasant youngster.'

'He's a thousand years old.'

'Well, age is just a number …'

Jim's attempts to reason with Shelly were unhelpful as they started venturing from the point. Frustrated,

Shelly let out a rather beleaguered moan. She'd gotten off the same page as Jim and was looking to get back on.

'Get a grip, Jim. If we want to catch this Faye not-so-Friendly, we need to get a bit smarter.'

Jim placed his hand on Shelly's shoulder. 'Shell, I guarantee you, traps are like fishing. You can go all day without getting a nibble, but when you get that nibble, you have to be prepared to reel them in.' Jim turned Shelly around, noticing their dear old foraging counterpart Edna caught in a human-sized rabbit trap, trying her best to wiggle her way out.

'I've got a pretty good feeling that Faye not-so-Friendly is about to nibble.'

'Really?' Shelly asked.

'Aaaaaahhhh!' rang out another voice, one with a strong Irish twang.

'Really.'

The wait continued …

What's Your Story, Morning Glory?

In her little Adelong abode, Ivana Zbrenica was lazing about, reading Benoit Piccadilly's *The Telltale Tentracentron*. It had been a worrying couple of weeks for the retired lass, who'd spent sleepless nights concerned about the welfare of Faye Friendly. Faye seemed too good for the world of foraging, and Ivana knew she needed to ward her off this path, towards a less life-threatening endeavour such as crocheting or free solo rock-climbing.

Ivana knew all too well the dangers that Urban Foraging posed. She'd been a Forager back in the 70s, spending her time picking with a hippie commune. She trawled the fields for chestnuts, made daisy chains with her mates, and rummaged the odd piece of booty along the way. Her quixotic adventuring shaped her into the sunburnt raisin she was today; sunscreen being seldom seen on the scalps of Tumutians. It was fun, but as she would learn, ruinous for many.

On December 16th, 1979, Ivana was involved in the Great Morning Glory War. Having hoped to get high off of a few sprigs of morning glory, her commune was shocked to discover that their nearby field had been rummaged by a degenerate band of raiders. Their stash had been over-harvested, stripped dry, with not so much as a compensatory sprig left over for the hippies. It was a devastating scene to witness.

Angered, the hippies tracked down the raiders to nearby Kunama, engaging in a most lethal tête-à-tête. While reports about what exactly happened vary, the scene of the aftermath was horrific. Half the township had been burnt down, many had died gruesome deaths, and Ivana would lose both her right leg and her younger sister Marija.

This was unbeknownst to many in Adelong. She was seldom seen in anything other than long pants. It was a scar that harkened back to her dark past; a past she wanted to forget. However, as she glanced down at her exposed prosthetic leg, someone burst into her home. It was Faye, and she meant business.

'Ivana, I need to read your Foraging books, a …' Faye looked down at Ivana's leg, shocked by the sight. She'd never seen Ivana without pants and had no idea that this was a scar she wore. 'Uh …'

'My girl,' said Ivana as she sprung up out of her chair, 'this is what could befall you if you continue this urban foraging charade.' Ivana grabbed a nearby blanket and covered the abomination. She always had a spring in her step, but many figured this was her natural buoyancy and not the blade-like prosthetic she wore for exercise.

The silence lingered for a second. 'I think the foragers are after me, Ivana.'

'Didn't I tell you, silly girl, this is a dangerous game you're playing?'

Ivana raced over to her bookshelf, grabbing a copy of Benoit Piccadilly's *Pickled Dill*, a graphic depiction of the Great Morning Glory War of 1979. The book was covered in cobwebs, bound by strong twine. The pages were barely hanging onto the spine, but they held together well enough for this girl in quite the bind.

'Read this my girl, and these.' Ivana grabbed several more books; the seminal works of Benoit Piccadilly, the foreboding yet barely legible musings of Dilanthanaweera Diplendriademico. She wanted Faye to know as much as possible to prevent a catastrophe from reoccurring.

Faye tried her best to juggle the pile as Ivana continued to load her up with literature. These books consisted of cautionary tales, letter collections, erotic fiction, biblical prophecies, advertisements, and a scratch-and-sniff booklet that Benoit Piccadilly had compiled during an experimental phase of his career. While scant on actual content, Faye hoped to parse through some of the knowledge wedge between the Danoz Direct ads and haikus.

Faye sat down and began flicking through a few of these books, browsing the passages and perusing through the prose. She was desperate for one of these books to supply salient advice on how to defend yourself against no-goodniks. She read through the softcore erotica, trying her best not to gag at the sordid depictions of custard apples being inserted into various nether regions. These books were revealing, but more of Benoit Piccadilly's warped psyche and broken home. Seeing these as useless, she moved on to more pertinent books.

After a good twenty minutes of reading, Faye closed her current book and looked towards Ivana. 'I need to know how to defend myself.' She threw the pile to the ground. 'These people are after me, and I don't know why.'

'What did I tell you girl? This is a dangerous game.'

'But I'd always thought of Foragers as a bunch of nice old people picking plants and being self-sufficient. Why are these people such freaks?'

'I'll tell you why, my girl.' Ivana once again pointed down to her prosthetic, proceeding to tell her story. 'Greed. I was just a young lass without a care in the world. I had a basket full of Bergenia, the bouquet of dreams. I had the whole world in my hands. I thought I'd found my community. Then one day – as a wild walkabout stood over me – a deranged young lady gnawed my leg off, all for a few bloomers. I knew that this pastime was the avocation of savages.' Ivana took a sip of her less-than-authentic Croatian coffee. 'These are feral people, my girl, you shouldn't be stooping to their level.'

'Then how should I proceed? How do I destroy these pricks.'

Ivana sighed, knowing she had to bring out the big guns. She signalled for Faye to follow her through the kitchen. It was unkempt like a six-foot-long beard. Ivana was usually a little OCD about the state of her kitchen, keeping it as spotless as a panther.

'Sorry about the mess, my girl, but I've been so verklempt about this whole situation.' Faye nodded and continued following Ivana outside, waded through the overgrowth. The grass fluttered like green waves, small bugs flicking out like water droplets smacking against a boat. Her whole house was in quite the state, a worrying sign to say the least.

Ivana spotted something out of the corner of her eye. 'Fucking hell, these fucking …' Without hesitation, she picked up a stray red-bellied black snake, swung it like a lasso, and cracked its spine against the shed. Faye let out a gasp.

'Don't fret my girl,' said Ivana. 'It's one of the few positives I learned from that fucking life.' She chucked the snake aside, before proceeding to slowly open the shed. Plumes of dust seeped out, causing the two to cough.

As their eyes adjusted to the dim light inside, what Faye saw in front of her was a sight to behold. It glistened from the natural light, oscillating ever so slightly. It had a mystical, unnerving presence about it, more at home in a fantasy novel than a shed in Adelong. Faye's eyes dilated; her jaw dropped. It was possibly the most beguiling thing she'd ever seen.

'Is that …?'

'Yes, my girl.' Ivana put her left hand on the right shoulder of Ivana. 'They won't fuck with you if you have this, my girl.'

'Really?'

'Really. I've survived 40-plus years with this in my possession. That's a miracle with my past.' In front of Faye appeared to be the fabled Golden Clover of Finnlaigh Cumlach. Many thought this was a mere urban legend designed to create an uptick in the local tourism industry. With its shiny exterior and incalculable value, many have sought this out as it promised everlasting life, prosperity and better luck with the opposite sex.

But this raised bigger philosophical quandaries. What powers did it really possess? Was this a stabilising force in the geopolitically contentious Snowy Valleys? Was it really beneficial to male fertility as Finnlaigh and his 23 children have attested to? These were questions Faye would have to reckon with.

'Now, I want this to be yours, my girl.' Ever so gently, Ivana picked up the Clover and proceeded to place it in Faye's front shirt pocket. 'To take these pricks on, you should carry this with you. If nothing else, they won't fuck with you anymore. They may want to fuck you, sure, but I'll leave you to choose who you seek courtship with.'

Faye peered inside the shirt pocket, once again in disbelief. With a lethal tête-à-tête in her near future, she needed any help she could get. Ivana was old and frail, Damon was gangling and impish. The rest of her friends had lives. If this Golden Clover gave her a modicum of luck going forward, she would take it.

In the Horny Goat Weeds

Beleaguered and verklempt, Jim and Shelly sat back-to-back on a dirt mound in the forest. Like a symphony of agony echoing around them, the dozen or so people who'd fallen into these traps were begging to be freed. To an untrained ear listening, this would seem like the inside of a deranged and illegal torture chamber like Guantanamo Bay post 9-11. Cries for help, pleas for forgiveness. All of this rang rowdy in the ears of Jim and Shelly.

Nevertheless, they were motionless. Simmering doubts over the futility of their foraging governance were starting to seep in, like a cool draft through the walls of a decrepit old homestead. No one took them seriously, fewer actually cared. It was all a bit too much for the rancid old foragers. A career in sales seemed like a more pleasurable way to spend their next 30 years, as opposed to this forest-bound actuality.

'We tried raising attention,' Jim bemoaned.

'Warning the masses.'

'The unwashed asses, of this societal scourge.'

'The woman on a purge.'

'But they didn't listen.'

'Advice they wouldn't heed.'

'Indeed.' Jim took a hit of his snuff, an organic substance that foragers often warned others not to use as the risks involved were grand. Over the years, he'd handed out many infringement notices to youngsters trying to get enough of the snuff. With the hallucinogenic effects starting to kick in, he felt he could fly, worrying Shelly. However, his gazing upon the stars was the least of her concerns.

Shelly groaned, playing with a nearby stick. 'This is your fault.'

'WHAT!' Jim sprung to his feet. 'How is this my fault? I was trying to exercise my jurisprudence by cracky!'

Shelly stayed seated, flicking away an ant, the last remaining ant from the colony that had been eviscerated by the hellfire and fury of Former Luland's viscus and mucus firestorm. The courageous young ant had been desperately looking to escape the chaos, traversing the gruelling terrain that was the forest floor. It had made a harrowing 100-meter trek over the past two hours, avoiding the ever-present danger of feet, phlegm and flies. As freedom was mere moments away, it was squashed by the stick of doom, wielded by Shelly, in her moment of severe malaise.

Disregarding her own callous ant murder, she half-heartedly turned towards Jim. 'This is changing you, Jimothy.'

'How?'

'You're willing to disregard your jurisprudence, to let ne'er-do-wells break the law, all because you want to bring this bitch down.'

'That's preposterous, my love.'

'Yeah, you disregarded a tip-off from that young lad reporting Luna Zukas's illegal treading on the endangered White-Knuckled Lily Flower.'

'I mean … you can't expect me to try and reprimand the First Lady of Tumut over an innocuous flower stomp?'

'You had no issue apprehending the Chief Police Officer of Tumut.'

'Headingly had it coming.'

'Yeah, like the ones in the—'

'Uh buh, buh.' The two pressed their fingers into each other's faces, a rare argument from their 22 years of marriage. Often in sync with their bizarre and eclectic behaviour, arguments only occurred when their values were truly compromised. The bliss of their matrimony had carried them this long, but with tensions lingering under the surface, this bliss could be pissed away all thanks to Faye Friendly.

'Are you really going to let this ruffian do this to us, my love?' Jim turned away, grabbing a few sprigs of Eucalyptus from a nearby gum tree. 'Shelly, I love you more than life itself, and this moral quandary isn't going to dampen that spirit.'

'Isn't it?'

'No … my love.' Jim proceeded to crush the eucalypt between his teeth, before planting a kiss on Shelly's lips. It tasted mouldy, like a mushroom left to rot in the back of a fridge. For most, this would be revolting and potentially life-threatening. For Shelly, however, this got the pheromones racing like a dolled-up V8 around Bathurst.

The two were locked in a sensual embrace, the earthy aroma a turn-on for both parties. The tongue came out, and Shelly proceeded to suck on it. Not even the Dalai Lama would approve of this tongue suckage; it was too gross for human consumption.

It was also annoying for nearby Murray Lefebvre. A local councillor who had a secret compulsion for poo jogging, he'd ventured into these woods to get his cardio in and last night's Tikka Masala out. Having become ensnared in one of the many traps of this forest, he was looking to be freed, not only from this trap but from this revolting practice of eros.

'Come over here you freaks, free me dammit.'

'Oh, I'm coming alright,' Jim said, before swooping Shelly off her feet. 'I'm ready to treat you right, my love.' The two continue making out, Murray Lefebvre letting out an audible groan. At that moment, Benoit Piccadilly's experimental pop song 'Everyday is Like a Sunflower' – Murray's ringtone – began ringing. It was the perfect mood setter for the two foragers, and with Piccadilly's baritone voice ringing through the shrubbery, the two began rooting on a pile of dead roots.

This went on for several minutes, Piccadilly's introspective musings on sexual longing and depression ringing hollow as Jim and Shelly ploughed each other senseless. With a crowd of ensnared Tumutians watching on, the two painted the forest a variety of colours, most of which blended into the greenery like oil on water. Whatever the Tumut faithful did to deserve this wasn't clear, but neither was whatever lurked under the thick brush beneath Shelly's underwear. How Jim found his way in was a miracle, and with the right people watching, he could most certainly find his way on a survival show, telling the harrowing story of how he survived the harsh, arid climate that was Shelly's nether regions.

With a definitive grunt, Jim finished up, his seed burrowing into the earth, yet not promising to his hopes of sprouting new life. This was their first proper tryst in a long time, and with Jim's questionable hamstring, it would be their last for a while.

Although it was a most horrific sight for those watching on, it was even more cataclysmic for the sole surviving ant from the colony. The youngling had ventured off to meet up with the other surviving ant. Hoping to find its mate alive, the antling made the hopeful journey towards safety. Those hopes and dreams were promptly crushed by the thick, ropey vengeance that shot out of Jim like a bullet to the heart. Needless to say, it was a dark day for Tumut's ant community.

'That was magical,' Jim exclaimed.

'Mystical.'

'A moment to remember.'

'Something we'll never forget.'

'Said that right asshole.' Kenichi moaned in his woozy haze; still somewhat conscious despite being fully stuck to his glue trap. Weary from his entrapment, Kenichi proceeded to place his head down for some shuteye. This was a bad mistake, as the side of his face became stuck in the glue, leaving him in an even more awkward position than before.

The two proceeded to fall asleep in each other's arms. It was romantic; tragic to say the least. It was the best they'd felt in quite a while. Not even a newly developing itch drowning out the sexual ecstasy.

If the tête-à-tête was encroaching, they needed this to realign the mind and soul. Whether that happened was debatable, but the orgasm was good nevertheless.

SUBMERGE!!!

Faye emerged from her little shoebox apartment on Simpson Street having prepared for an ominous day ahead. She'd spent the night reading the literature, perusing the pages of peril. Having completed the laborious task of parsing through the softcore erotica, she'd gleaned some pretty handy tips for dealing with these foragers. She'd learn about those who exercised jurisprudence, who scoured the streets for scavengers. Their totalitarian rule had created an enclave of freaks unwilling to let budding foragers try the hobby.

She was going to put a stop to it. Armed with a cheese knife, a peashooter, the Golden Clover and a treasure trove of knowledge, she stood ready for what lay ahead. The sun seeped through the vibrant autumn foliage, creating a dramatic vista of Tumut. Stunning, picturesque, a picture of the fall. It needed to look pretty, as trouble was about to call.

As she wandered, she noticed the usual sight of Submergist activist picketing. The lack of energy and poorly designed signs signalled another bit of rabble-rousing about nothing. After months of peaceful demonstrations and the odd egging, the likelihood of this ending in a necklacing was about as likely as a former mayor coming back from the grave. While it had happened once before, the weather and the crowd didn't warrant a resurrection.

However, there was a slightly different atmosphere in the air. There was a bit more vitriol behind the chants, a few more flares were set off. As dissenters made their way through the streets of Tumut, a certain hush was palpable; a forthcoming trouble brewing like yeast in a distillery. These folks had been protesting for years, not letting their hopes of a seafaring society sink. Despite a slew of rejections from multiple governing bodies, they were still persistent in realising their underwater utopia. With a hope for a better life resting at the bottom of a pond, they were ready to reel it in.

They made their way towards the centre of town. With pickets hoisted and torches lit, they wanted answers. Similarly, Faye made her way to the *Bean Flick*, where she could observe the political rally first-hand over a matcha. It was a small, yet vocal crowd; 60-ish people mostly over sixty. Fists were raised and scuba masks were worn. It was a good chuckle to anyone with a functional brain, and Faye certainly saw the humour in it.

'Faye, are you ok?' Damon asked as he brought her order to the table. Following the bounty hunter incident, he'd spent the last few days concerned for her wellbeing, his pre-prepared speech asking her out not on the forefront of his mind for a change. With his feelings for Faye still strong, he was naturally concerned.

She merely nodded 'thank you', her eyes locked on the rally outside. Her gaze followed a group of people wearing a half-baked cardboard cutout of a submarine. With a few cheap upgrades to the suit and a new video game controller to navigate the depths of the ocean, they could market trips to the future Tapat for a hefty fee. It was even bandied around by several prominent Submergist after hearing of an American billionaire taking people to see the *Titanic*. Unfortunately, a recent tragedy prevented the billionaire from answering the call of these folks.

Damon was about to turn and go but didn't. 'I've been worried sick about you.'

'Damon, I'm fine,' Fay snapped before taking a sip of her matcha. It was almost as if this run-in had empowered her. She wasn't going to take crap; she was in charge. 'I can handle myself, mate.'

Damon glared at her – wondering if he should press further – before leaving her to her own devices. This was certainly an odd turn of events, Faye's bubbly demeanour turning flat like days-old coke left in a hot ute. It did little to help him build courage for an eventual date request.

The crowd outside started firing up.

'SINK OUR SHIRE, DROWN IT OUT, THE TAPAT WAY, NO NEED TO POUT!'

It didn't have the catchiness of a Barmy Army Chant, nor did it have the rhythm of a well-rehearsed choir. The Submergist movement may be well-funded and highly motivated, but their penchant for lyricism had left them like a flock of birds before a hurricane.

It seemed like this was going to be another protest that meandered for a few too many hours without achieving anything. However, before these elderly seagazers got too bored, a cavalcade of cars arrived before them. With a particularly rowdy lot protesting today, the council had been forced to act on several complaints from nearby residents. It was highly unusual for the council to receive so many complaints, and even rarer for them to act on it. With nothing better to do, they decided to put the chess pieces down and travel down to the main street to suss it all out.

Stepping out of his stylish Honda Civic, mayor Phuck Whitton arrived. Flanked by the missus – the enigmatic Luna Zuka – he made his way to the front of the crowd. A tall, imposing figure with a pearly white smile, Phuck was quite the aspirational politician. Tumut was only a mere stepping stone for bigger things. A state senate run was to come first, followed by a crack at the House of Representatives. Once he bided his time in a cabinet position for two to three years, he was to attain the Prime Ministership, becoming a Howardian figure to the Australian populace. But first, he had to deal with the aggrieved Tumutians and their desire to create a land down below before he could conquer the land down under.

With his hand making a loose fist and his thumb pointed down, he addressed the crowd, 'Ladies and gentlemen, I implore you to remain calm!'

The crowd was loud and most certainly fired up, Whitton's presence was about as welcome as Chris Hanson on a date with your online girlfriend. A suspected Maoist spy, Whitton had received quite a hard time from the ardent Submergist. He'd been spat on, shat on, a meat pie mashed into his face. He'd been referred to the FBI, the CIA and the X-Files; the latter disappointing to those making the claim upon discovering that this was just a television show and not an official governing body.

Despite the hostile reception to his presence, Whitton persisted. 'I understand your concerns; however, I disagree with your methods.'

'Shut the fuck up, dickhead! – 'No one voted for you, cocksnap.' – 'Maoist land shill' – 'Go home, tosser!'

Whitton tried to command their attention, but his efforts were as futile as a trip to the moon in a bottle rocket. The Submergists were steadfast in their methods and continued hurling both insults and projectiles at the mayor.

Luna Zuka, who'd been in the car gorging on Korean barbeque, was disgusted by the impish nature of her husband. A cowardly figure, Whitton wasn't one to stand up for himself. Mayoral rival and ex-mayor Dickhead Derrigan had once challenged him to an arm-wrestling contest, which he refused by purposely avoiding Derrigan for the next several weeks. If he acted this way towards drunk town mayoral candidates, he could find himself in a spot of bother when he enters the Australian Senate.

With her man cowering to the mob, she knew she had to act.

'Gosh, this is unbelievable.' She stepped out, her fur mink coat blowing open to reveal an expensive blue dress with a photo of her face embroidered onto it. Her vainglorious nature was quite confronting to many, including her husband, who often had to pick up the tab for her decadent lifestyle.

'You're interrupting my day.' Not only was she sick of the continued protests from the Submergists, but she also detested her husband being a wimp to anyone giving him a bit of lip.

She kicked her husband to the side and addressed the town. 'I'm sick to death of you pricks continually blocking our paths and disturbing the peace. Anytime I go to eat kimchi, I hear you pricks ranting about The Callum the Tsar or whatever his name is. I've had enough.'

Amidst the confrontation, Faye had slipped out to get a closer look. Leaving her matcha unpaid for, she hastily worked her way towards the crowd, wanting to catch Luna losing her shit. This caused further concerns for Damon. Not only was Faye always good with paying, but she was a prodigious tipper. A five-dollar cuppa usually cost Faye a tener; a token of her immense gratitude. Money was nice but the change in behavior was more worrying.

As Faye got closer, she heard the argument between Luna and the leader of the Submergist movement, Fannie de Hamza. The woman wore a SUBMERGE shirt, complimenting the daisy chain around her neck.

'I'm tellin' ya commies, submit to the sink, there is no hope.'

'Listen here Fa-nye. I don't want to grow gills; my lungs are fantastic, thank you. I suspect no one else in Tumut wants to grow gills either. Go away.'

Fannie wasn't going to take no for an answer, offering an alternate way of life to the first lady. 'Have you ever considered seafarin' life deary? For your walk-in wardrobe to be Davy Jones' locker?'

Luna lingered on that thought for a fleeting moment before snapping back, 'I've considered clocking you, to be frank.'

The proceedings were getting testy. Luna wasn't budging, and neither was Fannie. A tête-à-tête was brewing, and they needed someone to split the tension. As a cold breeze enveloped the air around Tumut, something emerged from the doldrums of history which was through the drive-thru of the local McDonald's nearby.

'Aye,' said a voice from atop a horse. It had a particularly noticeable tone; almost like watching an archive video from the 1930s. The people turned around, and the audible gasps of the Tumut faithful swallowed the air in one foul gulp. Faye's jaw was also on the floor, as she stared at a figure seemingly lifted from a history book. This was surely a ghost, right?

'I have   arrived   ,' proclaimed none other than Finnlaigh Cumlach. The ex-mayor of Tumut didn't look a day over 40, stunning considering he'd not been seen in over a hundred years. It could very well be the biggest endorsement of modern anti-aging methods yet. The man exuded a sexual charisma, several elderly ladies in the crowd biting their lips, pheromones racing at the sight of this 140-year-old spunk of the Snowy's. Artistic interpretations of the man proved not to be the hyperbolic fantasies from bored housewives who took up art as a hobby. Although anatomically speaking, some artists were underselling what he had packing in his pantaloons.

However, Luna wasn't as versed on the history of the Snowy Valleys and couldn't immediately recognise the almost mythical figure. Pushing one of the protesters aside, she stepped towards the former mayor.

'Who the fuck are you?' she politely inquired.

'Finnlaigh Cumlach, I used to be the mayor around these parts.'

'Well, you're not now, fuck off!'

Finnlaigh was taken aback. 'You don't want to hear the stories about how I managed to live over 140 years? How did I manage to elude my political persecution?'

Luna scoffed. He may have been the mayor during one of the most turbulent times in Tumut history, but he wasn't now.

The Submergist faithful were a little keener to know this man's story. He was an urban legend to many, and his story needed to be documented in full.

'Go on,' they said in unison.

'Don't go on,' Luna said, wanting to deal with this before her forthcoming nail appointment.

'So, you don't want to hear my fabled story?'

'I don't. I need to drink champagne and look gorgeous. Go away!'

'Unbelievable.' After a hundred years of hiding, Finnlaigh figured someone would want to hear him regaling his tale. He was thoroughly disappointed.

'It is unbelievable Fine-leigh.' Luna then turned her back to the man, returning to the argument she'd been engaged with.

Considering a return of such grandeur, Finnlaigh was rather offended by such a cold response. Wanting the attention for himself, he decided to bring out the big guns.

'So I guess you don't want to see the Golden Clover?' The crowd gasped as Finnlaigh hoisted the mythical item above his head like a dagger about to strike the heart of a human sacrifice. It shimmered, sparkled, trappings for one's eye. Everybody knew what the Golden Clover was and wanted it like a kid wanting toys at Christmas.

However, this confused Faye to no end. She'd just been given the cloverleaf from Ivana. It was in her pocket, a lucky charm on her perilous journey. Who was this blow-in sporting his supposed cloverleaf?

'Nuh-uh, I've got the cloverleaf,' said Faye, hoisting her leaf in the air. The crowd turned to look, significantly less impressed by her version of the Golden Clover. It didn't have the pizzaz, the grandeur, the sparkle that Finnlaigh had. It was almost as if it was a cheap counterfeit.

'Oh,' said Shiralee, owner of a local crafted goods store, 'those are like the ones I sell, so glad you bought one. You're doing your bit to help small businesses.'

Faye was in disbelief. She'd been sold a bill of goods by her close friend Ivana; swindled, scammed, flimflammed. She looked like a right goose in front of the Submergist movement, a movement priding itself on being a geese like people.

'Everyone here is fucked,' Luna said, walking away with her impish husband. She'd had enough, and for all she cared they could tear each other apart like feral dogs. She had a wine with her name on it and couldn't take any further whining from the Tumut faithful.

Faye was left standing there, embarrassed, shocked. In her moment of solitude, Damon emerged from the masses, attempting to be a voice of reason.

'C'mon Faye, let's get out of here. I need to ask you something.'

However, before she could move along, one man stepped up.

'Isn't that the lassie with a bounty on her head?'

'The woman that those want dead?'

Faye's anger turned defensive, and in a rather unexpected moment, snapped.

'NO NO NO. I'm not letting you absolute fuckwits …'

Damon whispered a gentle plea to his fired-up crush. 'Faye, don't swear.'

'… fuck with me. I've had some fucking freaky fucks following me because I pick a few stray flowers occasionally. Fucking criminal I am? I've fucking had enough. Fucking come at me.' Seemingly broken in her embarrassment, Faye stood toe to toe with the Submergists, ready to take them on. Forced into battle by the machinations of the Urban Foraging community, she was ready to take up arms like Afghani women defending their settlements from an ISIL invasion.

Damon was really concerned about this. His suspicions were proven correct, something had changed with Faye. This wasn't the friendly, caring lass he admired; this was a soldier prepared for battle. With a cheese knife in her left hand and a peashooter in her right, she was ready for a war Damon wasn't prepared for.

'Just think about this for a moment dear.'

'Fuck off Damon, I have to take care of this.'

Damon stepped back. With a deep breath, Faye pointed the peashooter at the nearest Submergist agent.

'Wait,' Finnlaigh shouted, 'you've had issues with the foragers?'

Faye turned to him, an eyebrow raised. 'Yes.'

'I've had my issues with one of them, deary!'

'Really?'

'Indeed! I'm just going to get back at one of them now, wanna join?' Finnlaigh extended a hand, which had a certain mystical hue radiating off of it. This could just be 100 years' worth of not washing, but this seemed a bit more mystical than your stock standard hand rot. Slightly less putrid too.

Before they could trot off, Damon found it strangely appropriate to call out to her.

'Faye, before you go, can we talk? I think I need to tell you something?'

Faye looked his way, but just shook her head. All he wanted was to ask her on a date. He'd bottled this up for ages, and with an uncertain future ahead, he just wanted to hang out.

Despite a fleeting moment of hesitation, she took Finnlaigh's hand and he hoisted her onto his horse. Once fully mounted, Faye signalled for Finnlaigh to ride off. With a kick of his heels, the horse began trodding off, the Submergists left confused by this whole sight. With nothing to do, they slowly restarted their chants, a more placid type of peace disruption than before. With Faye disappearing down past the pub, Damon felt like he was hung out to dry. As the Submergists slowly retreated past him, he just stood there watching Faye ride down the main street of Tumut.

Calm before the Storm Cloud

While carnage threatened to spill onto the streets of Tumut, carnal desire had enveloped the sweaty embrace of Jim and Shelly. For the past day, they'd painted the forest different shades of grey, brown and red. While those ensnared in their traps had fallen asleep, they'd been fucking like rabbits, going through all the positions listed in Benoit Piccadilly's *The Telltale Tetracentron*. They were spent, and after such an intense bout of lovemaking, they decided to rest in each other's sweaty embrace.

They both stared at the full moon, a most beautiful compliment to a crisp, clear night in Tumut. Through the fluttering gum leaves were the stars above heaven, trillions of light-years away. The rare bit of respite was a welcome break from their continued jurisprudence.

It was nice.

What wasn't nice, however, was the increasingly frustrating itch they were experiencing all over their bodies. It started on their calf muscles, but it was slowly rising up their bodies like a boa constrictor masticating their prey. An irritating sensation, the two started to scratch their itches, an ill-advised move considering what they'd been rubbing on themselves.

'A bit itchy love?' Jim asked, as he too started scratching up his arm. Skin was peeling, the patches of skin that remained turned red. These two thought they'd rid the forest of any invasive species that could cause such maladies. Nettle could stay, but if they were to encounter a stray Patterson's Curse or an auspicious Oleander, they were sent back where they came from like a far-right political slogan.

'I've been inflicted with a most dreadful rash,' Jim moaned, itching and bitching aplenty.

'Does the skin feel like ash?'

'Yeah, and I feel like ASS.'

'I've grown quite weary.'

'Try being strung up by the ankles, assholes!' Kenichi yelled, briefly brought out of his stupor, using this moment of awareness to make the sarcastic quip before falling back into a state of unconsciousness.

Thinking on his feet, Jim reached into his tote bag and pulled out a bottle of apple cider. It was a home-brewed remedy, and judging by the putrid smell, not a particularly well-made one. It was one of many things the two made themselves. Apple cider vinegar, urea, fertiliser, bags, even condoms. There weren't too many everyday items that Jim and Shelly couldn't crudely fashion in their home bathroom (except washing products, they'd evidently chosen to go all natural).

He proceeded to pour a little bit of this vinegar onto their respective rashes. This proved to be a terrible mistake, as the vinegar stung like a wasp caught in a beehive. The two screamed, a banshee-like wail reverberated throughout the forest and could be heard in nearby Rosewood. A very faint 'shut up' could be heard from the distance; however, Jim and Shelly chose not to respect this request.

This was opportune for one person who'd been wandering the forest at that time. Guided by the echo of this scream, this person waded through the shrubbery, over old stumps, and punji traps, perilously making their way to the location of Jim and Shelly. As they exited the tree line into the clearing, Jim and Shelly turned towards this lonesome wanderer. Their jaws dropped.

'My gosh.'
'The extreme pallor!'

'A man of valour.' The two foragers exclaimed as they looked at someone who might as well have been a ghost.

'Times up, scumbags,' said Harris Headingly, emerging from the tree line, his face illuminated by the nearby fire. The foragers stumbled back in horror.

The past few days had been rough for the police officer. He spent most of the first day cutting through his restraints, gnawing at the thick twine around his wrist. Once he'd freed himself, he then had to figure out how to escape. The minutes turned into days, and it was a wholly frustrating experience. He'd even resorted to drinking his own urine, which was immediately deemed unnecessary upon finding a bottle of Tooheys New in a filing cabinet. However, after taking a swig, he probably preferred the urine to the bottle of piss.

'I've got you now— Ahhhhhhh!'

In a cruel twist of fate, Harris Headingly had been ensnared in a well-placed snare trap. With rope tightening around his ankle and hoisting him into the air, his hopes of apprehending these wayward wayfarers were hanging by a thread, much like himself.

'Our time is up?'

'Yup.'

'The tête-à-tête draws near.'

'Our penchant for violence.'

'The silence in arrears.'

Headingly screamed, once again trapped by the two wayward wayfarers. 'Let me the fuck out, you overgrown freaks!' It had been a gallant effort to work himself out of his predicament. A book deal could've been made from this, an enthralling documentary with high production costs. His hopes of realising this were somewhat stifled by his second entrapment, to say the least.

'Don't pout.'

'The damned witch draws near.'

'Here here.'

'Tea, my dear?' Shelly handed Jim a thermal flask, an aromatic wattle-leaf tea warming them up. The methodical wait continued, along with their respective itches. Headingly was all but a brief scare in their campaign to reel in this existential threat. As he hung like a Christmas bauble, he was forced to suffer his cruellest fate up until this point; another round of Jimothy and Shelly's lovemaking.

A Lethal Tête-à-Tête

A lone parrot chirped in the desolate forest near Tumut. A chill swept through the air. As warned about in fables of the oft-forgotten past, a disturbance to the general order of things had brought the community to its knees. With its citizens in a state of unrest and its wildlife quickly following suit, the stage was set for a most lethal tête-à-tête.

Stationed behind their log were Jim and Shelly. The morning fog obscured the occasional glances they made from beyond the fallen oak. Their dedication to duty led them down a perilous path to perdition, their practice crippled by those seeking to destroy them. Their path to this moment was laden with traps, snaps, and a little bit of crap. With mushrooms between their teeth and fire in their eyes, they were ready for this tit-for-tat to end.

'Jimothy.'

'Shelly.'

'This is it.'

'Our tête-à-tête.'

'Born from a tit-for-tat.'

'From that dastardly rat.'

'She's wearing a hat!' said Jim, pointing towards a silhouette in the stirring fog … piercing the mist, Faye emerged, more armed than even the most weary forager. She was packing a punch. A Cursed Nettle net packed in her fanny-pack, a high-calibre peashooter holstered in her bandoleer with a poisonous minted pea serving as her artillery, industrial-strength glue and a highly potent South American pollen designed to make you cry and die, not necessarily in that order. To say she came ready for this moment would be an understatement.

And there was a man next to her. A tall, imposing figure, a ghost from the not-so-distant past. While Shelly was shocked, Jimothy was resolute, as if he were half-expecting this …

'Finnlaigh.'

'Jimothy.'

'Faye not-so-Friendly.'

'Weirdo.'

'Welcome to the tête-à-tête.' Jim stepped forth. He had been fixated on Finnlaigh. Jim knew him very, very well. They'd crossed paths many times before, despite the apparent age difference.

'You have … emerged, Mr Cumlach?'

'Indeed, Mr Jimothy?'

'Do you happen to have the cloverleaf?' Jim asked.

'The one you stole from me, hastening my demise?'

'That's not a pleasant attitude!'

'You've left people tongue-tied and twisted, lovers entwined, for picking fruits out of season?'

An uncomfortable silence lingered for a second, all three turning towards Jim as he tried to figure out a jocular response to such an inflammatory accusation.

'Well, Mr Finnlaigh, despite being dead for over a hundred years, you've certainly not lost your wit. But I see you have gained a cloverleaf.'

'I want the cloverleaf back.'

'Well, you stole it from me first,' said Finnlaigh.

Jimothy knew all too well what he was talking about. In 1917, Finnlaigh was waiting for the Luxembourgian delegation to leave town before emerging from his grave and reclaiming his mayoral title. However, that was all declared void when a young forager picked a shiny cloverleaf out of the ground. Finnlaigh was left to die a slow, agonising death, with about 49 years and 298 days worth of spam left. Some say that spam is the true lost treasure of Tumut, while others vomit at the thought of eating luncheon meat.

'Can we focus on the matter at hand?' said Faye. 'Why have you weirdos been following me, setting bounty hunters upon me? I just wanted to pick a few stray mustard greens, as a weekend pastime, and for whatever reason, you bunch of freaks have been on my back, stalking me at swap meets—'

'THIS ISN'T ABOUT THE MUSTARD GREENS!' Shelly snapped as she popped up from behind the log. 'This is about preserving tradition, heritage, respecting our elders, respecting the elderberry.'

Faye looked Jimothy square in the eyes. 'Is that why you've purposely obfuscated the secret of the Golden Clover from your wife, Mr Jimothy?'

'I, uh, yeah … like, I guess, well, if you see it from my perspective.'

'Jimothy, what is this roustabout blabbering about?'

At that moment, Finnlaigh took out the Golden Clover from his pocket. It had a hue about it, a shimmering light in a dingy, dark forest. It was gorgeous, magnificent! A sight to behold. It also held the secret to how you could look so good when you're so old.

Jimothy eyed the cloverleaf for a second, almost entranced by its mystique. Jimothy had kept a bit of a secret from Shelly. While forager lore stated that no secrets shall be kept, this one might have been better served as an unrevealed white lie.

'Shelly, how old do you think I am?' he asked. He took a moment to sit down back behind the log. His rashes were evident and he continued to scratch his arms with a fair bit of tenacity.

Shelly didn't really know how to respond. 'Jimothy, you're 62.'

'A fairly bad 62,' said Faye while she held a spade in her left hand. It seemed like it wasn't needed as Jimothy was digging his own grave. 'To be fair, I was skeletal at 62,' Finnlaigh remarked.

Shelly wasn't too impressed. Jimothy should be standing up for himself, seizing the moment and doing what he's been dying to do for weeks: hand Faye her rightful infringement notice. However, the appearance of Finnlaigh Cumlach was throwing the man for a loop.

She turned to Finnlaigh. 'You've spent a century not speaking, can you continue for another quick minute?' Whatever was happening, Shelly needed to get to the bottom of this. 'Jimothy, you're 62.'

'Shelly, my dear.'

'Here here,' Jim spoke out the side of his mouth, almost as if he were trying to obfuscate what he was trying to say. 'You can times that by two and add four.'

Shelly took a moment to do that math in her head. She murmured, trying to figure out why she was getting 246. She wasn't a wiz with arithmetic and struggled when Kenichi hosted *8 out of 10 Foragers Do Countdown at Forager Trivia Night*. It caused friction within the group, as she would claim the game was rigged and that Kenichi couldn't do mathematics properly. With Kenichi strung up by the ankles, she couldn't lay the blame on him for her mathematical ineptitude.

Before she could figure out the answer, Faye blurted out the answer.

'128.'

'Indeed, I'm 128.'

A collective gasp was let out, including by some of the trapped Tumutians who were still conscious. Shelly herself was flabbergasted. This revelation seemed too silly to be true. She met him as a spunky 26-year-old foraging lemons from a tree out the back of the Uranquinty Pub. He looked a little older than his purported age, but his devotion to the world of foraging captured her heart and imagination. Their first sensual embrace, over a pile of zesty delights, was something only a young man could do. The way he picked her up and took her breath away was magical, even if it was a sour feeling for the poor neighbourhood cat that had to witness their first tryst. Most people his age should be in hospice care, not dealing with felonious filth like Faye.

'There's no way.'

'It's true, my love. I'm 128 years old. I've reached my golden years, and the only thing keeping me from growing old was that damned cloverleaf.'

'It's not bad, isn't it?' said Finnlaigh, as he inspected the leaf under the sunlight.

'You're not bad yourself, my feller.' Emerging from the fog was the devil himself, Slevin the Leprechaun. Having seemingly been MIA for the past week, Jimothy had presumed he'd taken their deal and spent it down at the pokies.

'My queen, my Sleve,' said Finnlaigh, his eyes filled with love, his pupils dilating wider than dinner plates. Slevin was now wearing a crown – the royal crown – that of the Luxembourgian monarchy. He wore a leopard-print dress, and a large diamond ring on his index finger.

'I've been waiting over a hundred years to see your face, my dear.'

'This is getting weird now,' Faye said.

Finnlaigh's eyes locked with Slevin's as they slowly walked towards each other. Their walk slowly turned into a gallop, before becoming a full-on sprint. They were ready to share their first sensual embrace for over a century – a love rekindled, a flame reignited.

'I love aaahhhhh—'

Unfortunately, as Slevin went to jump into the arms of Finnlaigh, he fell straight into a trap. The last trap that hadn't been set off; the punji stick plunge that'd sucked many a soul into the shitty beyond.

Finnlaigh stopped just short of the pit, peering over the edge. A bit below him was the lover he'd spent 100 years wanting to hold again. He'd faced the pesky dilemma of being dead, unable to break free of his casket. Despite this, he was unwilling to let the rot of time envelop him like your stock standard corpse. His soul yearned to be reanimated, just so he could nibble on his lover's ear one more time.

But now, after hundreds of thousands of hours, the lover he so desperately wanted to be with was now ten feet below him impaled with the shitty end of Jimothy's wrath.

'You monsters,' he uttered, fixated with what was at his feet. He grabbed a spade, snarled, and ran towards Jimothy. However, he forgot one thing that had been standing in the way of the two: the punji pit. He fell head-first into the abyss, killing him almost instantly. While this was an annoying way for his resurrection to end, he at least died in the arms of his long-lost lover

Slevin, even if there was a broken-off bamboo shoot sandwiched between the two.

This interlude was unexpected, and possibly unwelcomed. However, this now made way for what this was all leading to: the tête-à-tête.

Jimothy now found himself in quite the state. He was scratching and coughing uncontrollably, his age finally catching up with him. He had aged about ten years since this started, and it showed. His hair had greyed, his voice grew croaky. With the shrivelling of his testicles to top this off, he also felt a bit less blokey.

Despite this coughing, he tried to speak. 'Faye, not-so … Friendly …'

He waited for a second, expecting his darling wife Shelly to volley off his sentence. However, she stood with her arms crossed. Faye held a spade in her right hand and a peashooter in her left; a different war was brewing, however.

'Shelly, you're forgetting your …'

'You lied to me, for decades …'

'No, I told an alteration of the truth …'

'A lie …'

'No!'

Jimothy tried to rise from the log he was seated on but collapsed into a bundle of pain. 'AAHHH. AHH, SHELLY! WHY?!'

Despite his cries, Shelly was unsympathetic to her husband's pain.

'You lied to me!'

'This shouldn't be about the cloverleaf.'

'This is about trust.'

The two continued to squabble for a minute about the cloverleaf and his foregoing of the laws of foraging. It had been bubbling to the surface for a while but now it was all coming out.

Which gave Faye her chance to strike. With Harris Headingly strung up near her, she had wandered over to his location. She cut him free from his trap using the cheese knife. She knew this could happen. People within the foraging community were easily sidetracked. For instance, Benoit Piccadilly was known for going on many diatribes in his book.

From arguing that the Golden Wattle shouldn't be considered flora, to some troubling views on immigration rates, he couldn't always stay focused. This was a pattern across many foraging books, he could get distracted.

'Thanks, mate,' Headingley said, gracious of Faye's rescuing. After dusting himself off, he quickly sprinted over to the arguing.

'Your sweaty romance hasn't been that great for decades.'

'You don't even appreciate the reishi mushrooms I pick for you.'

'I hate you.'

'I'm arresting you two,' said Headingley, 'for false imprisonment, and by the looks of it, two counts of murder.' He pointed his gun at the two. Shelly raised her arms, but Jimothy protested.

'I've just been exercising my jurisprudence— Ahh!'

Jimothy grimaced and grabbed his leg, the pain of his rash now becoming unbearable.

'You have no jurisprudence!'

'How dare you!'

'Come with me, freaks!' Harris proceeded to handcuff the two. The tête-à-tête wasn't with Faye, as they feared. It was a more troubling tit-for-tat, with themselves.

As they walked off, Shelly turned to Faye, 'This isn't over.' Faye didn't hear this as Jimothy was still screaming in agony. As Harris hauled them away, Faye picked a few dandelions. This was over, and with a smirk on her face, Faye twisted and turned her day away.

Epilogue Part One: Court for the Courtesan

There was a disquieting hush in the courtroom. Thirty members of the community – long thought to be lost or to have moved town – were seated to watch the trial of Jimothy and Shelly. Having been made to pay for minor infractions, it was satisfying for those involved to see the two weirdos face the consequences of their actions.

In their quest to uphold peace, the foragers had committed innumerable crimes along the way.

Jimothy more so than Shelly, but she was no shrieking violet either. In a more barbaric time, they could be facing the death penalty. However, it seemed like a 20-year sentence was the worst they could expect. They counted themselves lucky, if only for the meantime.

Their actions were not well-received around town. They'd been shunned by the Tumut faithful, ostracised by the Council of Foragers. Even a lucrative bribe to Former Luland to write a fluff piece didn't work, as he ended up reaming them in an article titled 'Fuckwits Kept Me Chained!' He took the bribe regardless, losing it in a prized cockfight between famed French cock Le Freak and Harris Headingly's Brother Dick Headingly. Putting his money on Dick was a bad move, as he saw that money pissed away through a lost bowel movement from Dick himself, leaving him vulnerable to a pecking.

Despite having the Tumut faithful squarely against him, a rash-covered, wheelchair-bound Jimothy was determined to defend himself with a certain vigour, and had many notes prepared.

Settling in the dock, he cleared his throat. 'Ma'am, my job was to exercise jurisprudence in my community. The inherent dangers of foraging are too great for the civilian population to understand. They don't know what it's like to dalliance on a pale bed of poison ivy, to tango with the twines under the full moon. If I'm not afforded the ability to exercise my jurisprudence, then I fret to discover what our society will become.' Jim paused on that final point, believing this to be a rather profound statement to end on. In his mind, he'd been unfairly persecuted for simply doing his civic duty. If he isn't allowed to rule the forest with an iron pinecone or apprehend those who want to plunder the booty of hardworking Tumutians, then he's as toothless as a patient of Tumut dentist Izayah Yankem.

Unfortunately, the Tumut faithful were unimpressed with his final statement. Jimothy and Shelly were charged with 14 cases of false imprisonment, 175 historical cases of impersonating an officer of the law, 21 cases of theft and two cases of criminal negligence resulting in death and one case of coercion. While they could certainly empathise with the plight of someone trying to do the right thing, the line was crossed when you ensnare someone for picking a pheasant berry out of season.

The jury murmured amongst themselves as Jimothy finished. He looked quite proud of himself, as if he'd given the Sermon on the Mount and not a haphazard defence of his heinous actions. With a snicker, he felt victorious as if he'd pulled it off. Years of eating nothing but berries, bugs and the odd barbiturate had deluded his thinking. He was madder than a cut snake, but he felt like his argument had venom behind it.

'I now call on Miss Shelly to deliver her final statement,' said the judge.

The crowd hushed as Shelly slowly rose to her feet. In a zombie-like trance, she slowly sauntered over to the dock. She was a pallid ghoul, a shell of her former self. These last few weeks of captivity had been hard on her psyche, and this seemed to be her final chance at redemption.

She cleared her throat. 'Ladies and Gentlemen, I'm guessing you want me to make some grandiose statement about how I've been wronged, victimised, something or other.' She paused on that, as if waiting for someone to give a response. With the silence of the room crushing her yearning for validation, she pushed through. 'However, I have only one thing to say, and that is to Mr Jimothy.'

Shelly turned to Jim, her look changing from sombre to hatred in the blink of an eye. She snarled, 'Jimothy, I want a divorce, and I want one NOW!'

Jim gasped, as did several in the crowd. People who knew these two knew they were attached at the hip, bound by foraging lore. The people of Tumut expected a divorce like they expected to see a unicorn drinking from a trough in the main street. These two, for their many faults, were too perfect for each other. Sure, the last few months brought forth some trivialities, but not enough to end their matrimony, right?

The judge, Sheila Takabow, felt it necessary to interject. 'Miss Pecorino, I must inform you that this isn't the forum to initiate divorce proceedings, I must—'

'Shut up,' Jim shouted, in a fit of rage. 'Shelly, how could you?'

'Jim, when I married you over 30 years ago, I needed someone who knew how to forage my bush, to satisfy me with the mushroom of copulation, and who could properly protect the forest from plunder. Somewhere, somehow, in the midst of it all, you've lost your way.'

'I have not lost my way. If anything, I've become more pragmatic.'

'You let a bunch of white-toothed teens forage illegally, you've operated outside forager lore.'

'There were bigger fish to fry.'

'We nearly died.'

'I didn't realise we were servicing Venus on poison Ivy.'

'You wrapped your penis in it, honey!'

A moan of disgust rang through the courtroom, the visual of Jim's member wrapped in said plant causing several to reach for the vomit bag.

'I thought it was nature's condom.'

'ORDER!' Judge Sheila demanded, trying to regain control. But Jim and Shelly's gross argument continued for a further minute, getting stuck in the weeds over Jim's use of Horny Goat Weed. It was bitter, a result of many years of niggling issues. The argument wasn't too pleasant either.

Sheila bashed her gavel. It took a few seconds but it was enough to capture Jim and Shelly's attention, and Judge Takabow began delivering her final verdict.

'Look, it's abundantly clear to me that—'

'WE'RE GONNA SINK INTO THE GROUND,' a voice from the back exclaimed. This was Fannie de Hamza, *Clog Your Heart* owner and prominent voice in the Submergist movement. With little hesitation, she proceeded to rip off her top, revealing crude gills carved into her side. The crowd gasped, not just at her gills but at the crude winged eagle tattoo underneath her breast. Hansie was known for being a wild child in her youth, but this was quite the revelation even to those who knew her.

After a few seconds, the room was flooded by Submergist activists. They wore scuba masks, were shirtless, smelt bad, and had gills carved into the side of their body. For years, they'd tried to bring the Submergist movement to life. Several establishments around the region had been flooded or sunk into the ground. On this rather beautiful day, the Tumut District Court was just another one of them.

A burly man dragged a large firehose into the room, and with a turn of the nozzle, he began to turn the room into Davy Jones' locker. People scampered. Chants echoed off the walls.

'SUBMERGE, SUBMERGE, SUBMERGE, SUBMERGE!' The Submergist stood side by side as the courtroom became knees-deep in the essence of life. Doomed to a certain death in this small, stuffy room, the Submergists quickly realised their dream for a seafaring life was about to become their post-life regret. They'd be able to talk it out in another underground abyss – hell – to determine who exactly was at fault for their drowning. For now, they had to ...

'SUBMERGE, SUBMERGE, SUBMERGE!'

The last people left in this room were Jimothy and Shelly. For the last minute, both had been trying to unshackle themselves from these chains. Their attempts were futile; handcuffs had a different dynamic to vine. Their situation was grim, even disregarding the fact that they were surrounded by these Submergists; perhaps the only people in town who were bigger freaks than them.

'Quick Shelly, set me free!' Jim pleaded, turning his back to Shelly and holding out his arms, hoping she'd be able to loosen his cuffs. The water had reached their waist, they had little time to waste.

However, Shelly was willing to waste that time. She quietly hopped over to a nearby window. The glass was bulletproof and protected by thick metal bars, but Shelly hoped a lusty blow could bring her freedom. Coincidentally, with the lingering drug trafficking allegations levelled against several of these Submergist activists, a different kind of blow could have bought her freedom much more easily than what she was currently doing.

Once she'd reached the window, she tried to subtly bash in the bulletproof glass with her head, a predictably futile endeavour. Her blows were in sync with the rhythmic 'submerge' chants echoing throughout the room, adding some much-needed acoustics to the morbid acapella melody these damned souls were chanting.

'Save me, baby!' Jim pleaded, tears falling from his sunken eyes. Due to the amount of fungal bacteria on his face, the tears he spilt were having quite a chemical reaction. The stench that rose through the room hit the nostrils of all, causing the 'submerge' chants to be interrupted by bouts of coughing. Even though some Submergists were wearing scuba masks, they struggled to breathe with his newfound smell permeating the room.

'Save yourself from this damned damnation,' Shelly screamed before belting her head against the wall.

Jim tried treading water, which was now up to his chest, in an attempt to reach Shelly. In this chaos, Jim had an epiphany. Perhaps if he were to save Shelly, he could prove his loyalty, and this declaration of divorce could be rendered null and void like Jim's first marriage, a four-day affair with a Tarot reader named Gregoulie in 1976.

As Jim reached Shelly, he managed to bite her collar and pull her away from the bars. She struggled a bit, but with the symptoms of concussion setting in, she wasn't at her full capacity to fight back. After a minute, both managed to regain their composure.

'Shelly.'

'Dickhead.'

'Why won't you set me free?!' Jim asked with a wavering voice and tears in his eyes.

'Well, numbskull, that would be in direct violation of rule number 233 of Urban Foragers Lore, the very last rule in the rulebook: When the bomb comes, it's every man, woman, and tulip for themselves.'

Jim was heartbroken, dishevelled. His lungs may have slowly begun filling with water, but this was more tragic than that.

Bobbing above the rising tide, he pleaded with his darling wife. 'Baby, we still have hope!'

'Follow the rules Jimothy and SUBMERGE!'

Shelly joined in with the rhythmic chants of 'submerge' as they slowly ran out of air. A good few seconds went by, and the two sank underwater. Jim's tears mixed into the H_2O as he realised the futility of his life.

He'd spent his life steadfastly upholding the rules of society. If someone overharvested, they were apprehended. If someone was stung by a nettle, they were stung with a hefty fine. If they planted an illegal crop, they'd cop a spray. This dictum had been Jim's baby, his duty to uphold. The abidance of this very dictum had now led to his death. All he can do is SUBMERGE …

Epilogue Part Two: Jurisprudence

In her quiet little abode, Ivana Zbrenica watched the news, mortified by the events coming out of Tumut. Twenty-two people dead and the underwater mecca of Tapat not realised. Ivana was a soft supporter of the Submergist movement, but not enough to take a trip to Davey Jones' locker. She felt Tumut had run its course, but wasn't going to drown, of course! As these freaks submerged into their flooded graves, she felt comfortable eating a digestive biscuit and ordering more bottles for her collection.

Knock Knock Knock. She didn't expect visitors anymore. Faye had gone AWOL, and with no one to call, she spent her lonely days at home. She passed the time with art, yoga, and by making international roast coffee. Unless it was her late husband Bratka coming back from the dead, she didn't really want to see anyone.

'Unless it's you girly, I don't wanna know ya!' she grunted, changing the channel to watch the much anticipated *This Is Your Life* special for Larry Emdur.

'Open up.'

The voice was familiar. It was Faye who came tapping, tapping on Ivana's door. She was suited in full camouflage and had a high-calibre peashooter in hand. Ivana was relieved and quickly went to hug Faye.

'Faye, I'm so glad …'

'Ivana, have you read Forager Law?' Faye snapped back coldly. There was no joy in her eyes, no exuberance. This was a seriousness unbecoming of Faye. No longer the knockabout lass with a buoyant energy about her, she seemed like an entirely different person.

'Uh, girly, I—'

'Law 69: Never, and I mean never, give someone a counterfeit plant.'

Ivana stepped back as Faye raised her peashooter. She'd seen this before, specifically during the Great Morning Glory War of 1979. Faye had done her research, and this concerned Ivana deeply.

'Girl, I, look I just wanted to give you hope.'

'Fuck off.'

Ivana was now backed up against a cabinet in her loungeroom with all her green bottles in order but resting perilously close to the edge. Faye took aim. All

Ivana knew was that something was not right with her girl.

'I told you girl, don't get involved with these fucking …'

POP.

However, this lethal pea wasn't fired at Ivana, but at her prized collection. One green bottle fell, followed by two, then five, then ten … All Ivana could do was watch as her green bottle collection fell like Rome.

Faye watched on with a smirk on her face.

On the adjacent wall was a portrait of Humpty Dumpty, looking down with great disdain at Ivana who sobbed uncontrollably at the foot of her cabinet. She grabbed random pieces of glass, attempting to emulate the great egg himself and put them all back together again. As blood covered her palms and tears streamed down her face, she knew this was fruitless.

All that remained was one green bottle. Ivana was left wailing, her life's work shot down by someone she trusted. She knew the dangers that Urban Foraging brought. She knew what heinous crimes Jimothy and Shelly had committed. She'd hoped that Faye was to be a shining light in a room full of darkness.

Alas, it was not to be. Now, there was just one green bottle sitting on the wall. One young lass exercising jurisprudence over the Snowy Valleys. One fool left writhing in pain on the ground.

As Faye walked out of Ivana's house, someone was waiting for her. It was Damon Caruso, holding a bouquet. He'd had enough of his own lack of courage. He'd spent years wanting to ask this woman out. Many scrunched-up notes, clammy hands, and the odd visit to the local tarot reader. Damon was sick of his impishness. This was finally going to be the moment he pulled the pin and asked out the object of his desire.

With Faye stopping at Ivana's gate, Damon slowly walked up to her. His bouquet was filled with a whole assortment of flowers: roses, tulips, daffodils and daisies. It was a mishmash of colours that didn't really work together, but it was the thought that counted. Damon was sweating profusely, some last-minute doubts seeping into his soul. Faye glared at him, which didn't help his case. Nevertheless, he decided to man up and do what he'd wanted to do for a very long time.

'Faye, I want to go on a date with you,' Damon asked, offering the flowers. A year's long crush had led to this, the big date request. He shot her a smile, hoping she'd see how thoughtful this gesture was. However, his heart would be ripped to pieces mere seconds later through a sharp, stinging sensation between the eyes.

He fell to the ground, flower petals flying everywhere. He was dazed, confused. As his vision became less blurry and he looked up at Faye, he realised something that broke his heart: it was her.

'Law 54: Don't pick flowers out of season, failure to adhere to these provisions shall lead to a pea in the eye. Goodbye,' she said, before walking off into the distance, exercising her newfound jurisprudence.

Faye was once a model citizen to Tumutians everywhere, a person that old folks point to in order to shame their kids into getting better grades at school. Now, she had become something else.

Rubbing the spot between his eyes, Damon sobbed. To see the woman he'd been so infatuated with become this totally different person was heartbreaking. Seeing Ivana exit the house, he wiped his eyes and tried to hold back his tears.

Ivana sighed. 'I don't like her either …'